god

|||||||||||||||||||||||||||||||||

☞ **W9-AAL-679**

DEADLY SURPRISE!

Gracefully, I moved my hands to the center of my belt. It came unbuckled in my hand. Silently, I handed my rig to the bartender, who had been serving a table nearby.

"I'll be back for that, tomorrow," I told him.

I reached up and pushed at the doors, swinging them wide open. Someone yelled. A six-gun boomed, and a white-hot pain streaked across the top of my left shoulder. Sim was cursing, and his gun boomed again, this time missing me completely.

Whirling around, my hands reached out, and the derringers blazed away...

Also by Robert Bell
Published by Ballantine Books:

A VALLEY CALLED DISAPPOINTMENT

FEUD AT DEVIL'S RIVER

ROBERT BELL
Stranger In Dodge

BALLANTINE BOOKS • NEW YORK

Copyright © 1983 by Robert Vaughn Bell

All rights reserved under International and Pan-American Copyright Conventions. Published in the United States by Ballantine Books, a division of Random House, Inc., New York, and simultaneously in Canada by Random House of Canada Limited, Toronto.

Library of Congress Catalog Card Number: 82-90917

ISBN 0-345-30875-1

Manufactured in the United States of America

First Edition: May 1983

For Brett Barton
Edwards, 1887–1974:
cowman, philosopher,
and my friend. He was
as slick with a Colt as
any man!

CHAPTER ONE

THE COYOTE LIFTED his muzzle and sniffed at the scent of blood. Little eager yelps came from his open mouth, and he danced, nervously, his tail wagging. A few daring steps toward the huddled figure of a man lying silently beside the mounded embankment, and then a dash back to resume the frantic posturing. The dreaded man-smell terrified him, forcing him to keep his distance.

Four miles away in the hills behind him, his mate waited in their den with the three newly born pups. Weak from her ordeal, she was not able to help him find the food they both needed so badly. For two days he had gone hungry, while she struggled to give birth to that first litter. When this was finally accomplished and she was cleaning their firstborn, he had gone out in search of game.

A marmot's den had yielded nothing, and then he failed to run down a skinny jack rabbit that he had pursued for almost a mile. A whiff of this freshly spilled blood had been brought to him on the northwest breeze, and he'd homed on it unerringly. Now he sat, tongue lolling, beside himself with gnawing hunger pangs but held back by the hated man-scent.

The figure stirred, and the coyote's ears flipped forward for a moment, then lay back. He whined anxiously, watching as the bloody-headed man pushed himself to a seated position on trembling arms and leaned back against the embankment.

My head was splitting, and my ears rang. Putting a hand up to my forehead, I felt a flap of skin and hair covering my eyes. Through the excruciating pain I thought dimly that it felt as though a piece of my scalp was torn loose, hanging down in front of my face. Trembling, I used both hands to feel around and move it back in place.

With that out of the way, I lay still awhile. Then gingerly I rubbed my eyes. My vision was somewhat blurred but would improve. I was leaning halfway up against a railroad embankment, with the tracks stretched out in both directions. How had I gotten here? Again I kept still, not knowing what other injuries there might be. My head was still hurting, but I felt a little stronger. Perhaps strong enough to stand...

It took some effort, but I felt for the embankment supporting my back and forced one foot flat on the ground. By straightening that leg and locking the knee, I was able to stand, barely. My head spun a moment, then the dizziness passed and I saw a coyote leaving dust behind him. A rider was coming toward me at a steady lope. It was a man, and he reined in close by, whistling softly as he looked me over.

"Mister," he said. "Appears to me like you had yourself a tanglement, and you come out second best. What happened?"

By this time, I had started to look around, and I spotted a gouged mark in the gravel that extended for forty feet or more. Near the far end was a hat, and close by was a small, flat valise. With some difficulty, I walked over and picked the hat off the ground. Brushing it off, I gingerly tried it on over my lacerated scalp. It fit reasonably well, and I reckoned it would serve to hold things together anyway.

The rider stepped down off the horse and walked over to the gouge in the gravel. He reached down and picked up a few of the rocks....

"Blood all along this here track," he told me. "I reckon mebbe you fell—or was pushed—off the westbound. It barrels through here near about noontime." He looked me over a little more carefully.

"Mister, you'd best come along with me. My place is jest over that ridge you see there. My daughter is knowin' about cuts and bruises. You're bleedin' pretty bad. You crawl up onto this horse of mine, and I'll git on behind. You're gonna be bled out soon, if them wounds ain't taken care of. By the way. Don't recollect you tellin' me your name."

I stared at him! Suddenly I was very confused! I didn't *know* my name! I had no idea *who* I was! Nor did I have Idea One as to where I was, or how I had gotten here. The blood was running down the side of my face, and I brushed my shirt sleeve across my eyes and over my cheeks. It came away all soaked with crimson stains.

I spoke, haltingly.... "I...I guess I must have taken a bad knock, all right. I can't remember.... Don't know why I am here, or how it happened. Head hurts...." I slumped down to my knees.

"Water.... Sure could use a drink of water.... Throat's on fire, and my head does ache something fierce."

The stranger had gone to his horse, and now he uncorked a canteen and handed it to me. The water was brackish and a bit warm, but it was wet enough.

I took a second swallow of the reviving fluid and handed back the canteen.

"Thanks, mister. Tasted real good. I'm dryer'n a bone." I looked around, remembering the leather case I'd seen close to the hat. It lay there on the ground, dusty and all scuffed up from the gravel. Maybe it held some identification, or something that would give me a clue as to my identity, but right that second it looked mighty far away.

I looked down at myself. My boots were in good condition, though scuffed up like the case. My trousers appeared to be nearly new, so I wasn't in line for the poor house. Bemusedly I examined my right-hand pocket. It held some two dollars in change, plus a ten-dollar gold piece. I couldn't find a wallet, or anything with a name on it.

"C'mon, mister. Let's git you out of this sun. Can't be doin' you any good, with your head all banged up. Git up on that horse, and we'll figger out who you are later."

I nodded, and set a foot in the stirrup. He gave me some help and once I was firmly settled he retrieved the case and mounted up behind. The horse strained some climbing toward the ridge he'd pointed out, then we topped out a few moments later, and paused on the summit. Far as the eye could see was grass, and cattle dotted the landscape, everywhere. Hundreds of them!

At the foot of the slope was a large frame house, with a barn and corrals close by. Flowers, bright red flowers, grew in profusion around the fenced yard. This was no newcomer's outfit. These folks had been here for some time.

We came down the grassy slope slowly. My head was starting to spin again, and I grabbed on to the saddlehorn to keep from falling. We were nearing the house now, and I saw that a horse was tied near the front steps, and a man and a very attractive woman were on the porch. My benefactor had told me his name, Judah Clayton, while we came down the slope; a courtesy I couldn't return. Now, as he helped me down from his horse, he introduced me to his daughter and her companion. I was embarrassed, being so bloodied and all.

"This here's my daughter, Nancy. Nan, this feller's not in the best of shape, as you can see. He needs some lookin' after, so you take him on into the kitchen, and git out the medicine kit." He turned to the other man....

"Bill, I doubt this is in your jurisdiction, but somehow or other, this feller got himself pitched off the westbound today, and landed on his head. He can't remember who he is, or where he was headed." He reached up and untied my case from the pommel of his saddle.

"Found this valise, where he first hit the grit." Turning to me, he explained. "Bill, here, is City Marshal. In Dodge City, I mean. That's on down the line about eight or nine miles."

The marshal extended his hand. "William M. Tilghman," he said. "Let's go on into the house, and take a look at that head. You're sorta pale around the gills, and I ain't anxious to carry you in. You're a pretty big feller."

It was cooler in the house. I was feeling bad. Dizzy and sick to my stomach, I just wanted to lie back down.

In the kitchen they helped me out of my shirt, and Nancy poured a basin full of warm water from a pot on the back of the stove. Carefully, she sponged the crusted blood from my face and neck.

When they had taken off my hat, the loosened scalp had adhered to it and lifted free of my skull. Nancy had gasped, but she kept her composure and snipped the hair with a pair of shears from her apron pocket. "I'm going to give you a rather close haircut," she said. "I must, in order to sew the scalp back in place. Don't be worried. It will grow back, and you'll never see the scar."

Her father got a bottle of whiskey out of a cupboard, and poured me a glass half full. "Drink that right on down, son. Sewin' your hair back on may not feel so good. I can git you a stick of wood or somethin' to bite on, if you want."

I accepted the drink, and shook my head. "I don't guarantee I'll grin, but I will try my best to bear it."

The marshal was standing nearby, fingering the case, which lay on the kitchen table. He was a well set-up man perhaps six feet in height, with a large, dark mustache. About thirty years old, he carried himself with assurance. The walnut grip of a single-action Colt revolver protruded from a cross-draw holster on his left hip. As he leaned forward to examine the case more closely, his coat swung open, and I could see the gleam of a massive gold badge pinned to his vest.

He looked over at me. "Would you like me to try and open this?" he asked. "Mebbe there's somethin' inside that'd be some help in figgerin' out just who you really are."

"Go right ahead," I told him. "Of course, I don't really know if it's mine, though the circumstances seem to point in that direction." I winced as Nancy Clayton tugged my scalp back and took the first stitch high on top of my head.

"I'm sorry," she told me. "Perhaps if you had a bit more of my father's whiskey, it would lessen the pain."

"Thanks," I said. "But I'm already dizzy from that knock on the head. Another drink, and you'll be left with a drunk on your hands."

To tell the truth, I was already beginning to feel intoxicated. I was feeling warm now, and she had poured whiskey over the wound. The fumes were rising in my face, and they added to the liquor I'd drunk. Right now, all I could think of to help my condition was a nice hot bath. I even had the grit of gravel in my teeth. Plus I could feel twinges of pain in other parts of my body.

Tilghman was using a large clasp knife to pry the case locks. The first flipped out with a snap, and he grunted in satisfaction as he started to work on the second. It proved a little more difficult, but at last it popped open.

The marshal lifted the lid and whistled shrilly as the case's contents were exposed. "Well," he said. "Would you lookee here now!" He turned the case around so we were all able to see inside. I was dumbfounded! Nancy gasped again, and pulled hard on a stitch, bringing a yelp from me.

"I'm so sorry," she said. "It's just that I never..."

The inside of the case was lined with green felt. Set in formed recesses were six Colt revolvers. Three of them were Frontier models, with the three different barrel lengths. A pair of Lightning model double actions were nestled in there. One with the ejector, and the other without. The sixth gun, a long-barreled .38, had a picture of a thug and a policeman portrayed on the gutta percha grips. A Cop and Thug model.

Ammunition for all the revolvers was in boxes, along with cleaning materials and oil. On the inside of the lid was an inscription: COLT'S PATENT FIRE-ARMS MANUFACTURING COMPANY OF HARTFORD, CONNECTICUT. U.S.A.

"Well," said Tilghman. "It seems you're a sales-man for a gun company. Namely, Colt's. This has all the earmarks of a sample case. These weapons are all brand new, or nearly so. They show a bit of handling, but little else. Does this git any of the wheels in your head to turnin'? Do you recognize these beauties?"

I started to shake my head, then remembered Nancy's needle and thread just in time. "No," I replied. "I have no recollection of ever seeing those guns before. I know what they are, of that there's no doubt, but I don't remember selling them."

The marshal took one of the Frontiers out of the case. It had the shorter, four-and-three-quarters-inch barrel. "These are my favorites," he said. "The longer barrels don't count for a hill of beans in a gunfight. Fine for cavalrymen, when they take a rest over their saddles and shoot at Injuns a hundred yards away. The gunfighter's ranges are seldom more than ten. Main thing is to git it out, and start blazin' away. Even if you don't git a hit with that first shot, it's gonna bother the other feller's aim." He replaced the revolver in its niche.

I listened to all this, but had no comment. It did sorta sound familiar, but I couldn't say for sure. One thing for certain, I did recognize the guns as to models. It could be that I worked for the Colt Company. At any rate, it gave me a place to start searching for my identity.

Nancy had finished her sewing, and told me so. She wound a roll of bandage over a large pad placed over the top of my head, and secured it with a knot.

"There," she said. "All done. I doubt if Doc McCarty in Dodge City could do any better. Probably not as neat." She stepped back, and looked me over with a critical eye.

"I believe you could do with a bath," she told me. "Dirt is a deterrent to proper healing. Your clothes could stand a scrub too. You and my father are of a size, and I'm certain that he won't mind lending you a change until those are dry and ready. The wash house is out back. There are plenty of clean towels, so get along now. I'll fix you a bite to eat, as soon as you are cleaned up. Dad will bring you a change. Well! What are you waiting for? Do you want me to come and help you off with your things?"

I leaped to my feet, which didn't do my head any good.

"No, ma'am," I responded. "I'm on my way, right now!" The room spun for a moment, but I felt much better. I made them my excuses, and headed for the rear of the house. I reached for the door knob, then turned and faced my new friends.

"It's not really important, I guess, but what is the date today?"

Clayton scratched his head, and turned to Tilghman....

"Let's see, now. The election was April eighth. Hoover was elected mayor. He appointed you two days later, at the City Council meeting, and made Tom Nixon your assistant."

Tilghman was nodding his head. "I was ill with an inflammation of the skin, right after that, and Harry Scott had to fill in with Nixon. Wait a minute.... I was presented with this badge on Friday last, and that was May second."

Nancy spoke up. "It will take them forever to figure the date. Today is Wednesday, May seventh. Eighteen eighty-four."

CHAPTER TWO

BRIGHT SUNLIGHT IN my eyes woke me the next morning. The notes of a meadowlark came through the open window, together with the clang of hammer and anvil. I couldn't suppress the groan that came involuntarily, as I raised myself up in the feather bed. I hurt all over!

When I had bathed the day before, I'd found my body covered with livid bruises and welts. My elbows were all skinned, as were the points of my shoulders. I had apparently traveled the length of the forty-foot gouge in the trackside gravel upside down, bearing the brunt on my head and upper back.

The real shocker had come when I'd glanced in the mirror in the washhouse. I had stared at a complete stranger. No amount of warning could have prepared me for that. Plus I'd found scars—lots of scars. The largest, on my chest, fully three inches long and an inch wide, appeared to be from the stab of a knife. On my left thumb was another large, triangular scar, while a round, puckered mark under my left armpit was obviously from a bullet. I had no recollection of the wounds that had made them.

That face in the mirror was of a man, cleanshaven,

who appeared to be in his late twenties. The eyes were dark blue, almost black, and the hair was dark brown. The cheekbones and the jaw were heavily formed, and the mouth was wide and full-lipped. I looked to be just a trifle over six feet in height, and I guessed the weight at 185 or so. Apparently I'd led an active life, because there wasn't an ounce of fat on my frame. I sighed. It was frustrating not to know even who I was or where my family lived.

That hit me even harder! What if I was married? My wife would be wondering where I was, and would worry. No! She'd have no idea I was even missing. This had only happened one day ago, and no one would miss me, as yet.

Using the pitcher and basin by the side of the bed, I got my face and hands washed, and put on the pants and shirt I'd borrowed from Judah. I could smell ham cooking downstairs, and I was suddenly very hungry.

Nancy was standing by the cookstove when I came in to the kitchen, and she poured me a cup of steaming coffee.

"My father is shoeing a horse for you to ride," she said. "You might go on out there, and see if you can give him some help, even if it's only advice." She grinned...."You know, you look much better this morning. Almost handsome. Soon's that bandage comes off, you'll look even better. Now get on out of my kitchen, and make yourself useful. Breakfast will be ready soon enough, and I'll give you both a holler."

I thanked her, and took a cautious sip from the rim of my cup. "Hmmm! That sure does smell good! The ham, I mean. Can't remember when I've been this hungry." I smiled, ruefully. "Can't remember anything, as a matter of fact."

I went out and stood on the porch for a moment, enjoying the coffee. As I looked around, I could appreciate the care and the hard work that had gone into the building of Judah's place. He'd built hell for sturdy, and yet kept it pleasing to the eye. The flowers and the green grass—Nancy's share—were frosting on the cake. They set off the neat alignment of the whitewashed pickets in the fence.

An open-sided smithy sat next to the barn, far enough away that there was no danger of a spark's igniting the hay in the high-peaked structure. A blood-bay gelding stood there, one foot propped on Judah's chap-protected thigh. Using his farrier's knife, he was trimming out around the frog on that hoof.

"Can I give you a hand?" I asked.

He looked up, his face streaked with sweat. "No. I just about got it done. This is the last one. You can keep hold of that lead rope, if you like. This old boy's jest a mite fractious. He's been running barefoot for over a year. Fat and sassy right now, but he'll settle down. He's a fine one for takin' a nip out of my shoulder, or somewhere jest about as painful. Doesn't really mean any harm though. He started to develop some minor shin splints in April of last year. I'd jest got him to where he showed a lot of promise, but he was really too young to be packin' all my weight, so I turned him out with the colts. He's fine now! See! Not a sign of a splint!

"Now neither of us know if you've ever rode any kind of a critter, much less a trained cuttin' horse, but all this one lacks is exercise. So....You need a way to git around, and he has to build up his muscles. Fair enough?"

I agreed, and told him that breakfast wasn't too far off. As he unbuckled his chaps and got ready to wash up, I told him I'd just walk around a bit and get acquainted with the place.

"Fine," he replied. "Might jest as well put him out back in the small corral. We'll rustle you up a saddle, and whatever else you'll need, after we eat. I've got a few errands in Dodge, so we'll ride in together. Give us some chance to git better acquainted, and you can check around. Tilghman's plannin' to send off a wire to the Colt people, I believe." He handed me the lead rope, and I headed around the barn toward the corral, with the bay in tow.

After turning the horse in to the corral, I walked around a bit more, and found myself in a grassy clearing ringed by small, second-growth cottonwoods. Here, I found a heaped-up mound of earth, surrounded by human skulls. There were nine of them. A carved wooden marker was at one end, and deeply incised into the weathered surface was a date, June 8, 1866. ELIZABETH CLAYTON—WIFE AND MOTHER appeared just below.

I surmised that the skulls were those of Indians, but I'd no intentions of prying into Judah's grief. If he wanted me to know the details, I was sure they would be volunteered by either him or Nancy. Showed another side of Clayton, though; one contrary to his apparent mildness. Some of the skulls, one in particular, were not very old, while the others showed the sandblasted whiteness of the past eighteen years.

The clanging of a triangle announced that breakfast waited, and I'd best get going. Judah walked from the direction of the barn, and we entered the kitchen together.

The table fairly groaned from the weight of all the food. At Judah's end, a steaming ham waited to be carved, while in the center was a huge platter of beefsteaks. Eggs, with the yolks set just right, covered two platters, and potatoes, both fried and boiled, filled two big bowls. Biscuits, butter, and jellies were at each end.

Already seated were four young punchers and a white-haired oldster. Judah made the introductions, and they looked at me curiously but were friendly enough. Judah explained the bandage on my head, and they made some sympathetic comments.

Nancy brought over the coffee pot, and took her seat next to me, bowing her head for the blessing, which was given by Judah. I was embarrassed. I wasn't certain if this was done normally or not, but the others took it as a matter of course.

There was little if any conversation while the meal was being eaten. The silence, broken only by the click of eating utensils, continued until the food was all gone. I did more than my share of consuming the delicious meal, and I wasn't a bit sorry for it. Then, our coffee cups full, we leaned back.

When Nancy got up and started to clear away the dishes, I volunteered to help. She told me to stay right where I'd been. She could handle it by herself.

Then Bud Larkin, the older man who was Judah's foreman, started the conversation going....

"We've penned up almost two hundred young heifers in the high pasture, and I'd like to buy four small bulls to put in there with them. Small bulls usually mean small calves, and makes for easier birthin' with these first-calf heifers. We might check with that feller Hodgeman, over on the Pawnee. I heard he bought some Aberdeen Angus breedin' stock a year or two back. Got 'em from George Grant over to Victoria. Some of the stuff Grant brought over from Scotland, 'bout eleven years back. They're small, but the beef goes all the way to the ground. It'd mean a better calf crop, Judah."

Clayton looked up from the cigarette he was rolling. "We can ride over there tomorrow, if you like. I've been thinkin' on that myself, Bud. It's bad enough losin' the calves, but last year we lost a dozen heifers for the same reason."

One of the younger hands struck a match for his own smoke, and held the light for Clayton.

Leaning forward, he puffed on the cigarette, and squinted at me through the smoke. "You about ready to head in to the big city... uh, er... What the heck are we gonna call you? Doesn't seem right, you not havin' a handle. Makes it sorta hard to talk with you. Can't jest holler 'hey you,' when we want you to come." He thought for a moment....

"Got it! That there gun case you was packin'. From now on, that's what we'll call you. 'Case'! Nothin' wrong with a name like that. So, Case it is, until we find out different. That all right with you?"

I nodded. "Makes me feel better already," I told him. "I was feeling a little uncomfortable myself, with no name. We can get going anytime, Judah. I'm anxious to see if Marshal Tilghman has gotten an answer to his wire."

Nancy intercepted me on the way to the sink with my cup. "You just go ahead with dad," she told me. "When I need more help in the kitchen, I'll hire another Chinaman."

Judah stood in the doorway. "C'mon, Case," he called. "I gotta dig out a saddle for you. Let's git goin'!"

In a back corner of the barn was a small room, filled up with harness and leather gear. Judah pointed out one saddle on a rack to the left of the door.

"Go ahead and take that one," he told me. "I'll git you a bridle to match. You'll need a saddle blanket, so git one off that stack there. Go on out to the corral, and I'll see you there in a moment."

I carried out the saddle and draped it over the corral's rails. It was a long way from new, but it was well made and showed care. Clayton came out, carrying a rig for himself and an armload of other gear. He handed me a coiled rope, a pair of blunt-roweled spurs, and a saddle scabbard, with the carbine inside. It was a '73 Winchester. At one time, it'd been nickel plated, but most of the plating was gone. However, it was well oiled, and by the weight, I figured it was loaded. Jacking the action open partway, I found it so.

"Go ahead and dab your rope on that bay," he told me. "I got my horse on a picket back of the house. I'll be back in a minute."

Feeling none too sure of myself, I went in to the corral, building a loop on the way. The bay wasn't in a mood to get himself caught, but I trapped him into a corner and made my toss. The loop settled around his neck, and I drew up slack quickly. Once he knew he was caught, the horse settled down. Walking him over toward the saddle, I was startled to hear a loud whoop from Judah.

I looked around and there he stood, with Nancy standing next to him. He wore a wide grin on his face, and she looked mighty pleased about something.

"What'd I tell you?" he shouted. "He ain't no greenhorn. Did you see him ketch up that horse? Built hisself no more loop than he needed. Jest big enough to go over that bay's head. The horse knew it, so he didn't put up no fuss."

To further prove his point, he had me go ahead and saddle the bay. He was right! I did seem to know where everything went, so apparently I had done it before.

"Bought that saddle in Omaha," he told me. "Back in sixty-seven, I taken four hundred prime steers there, and sold 'em for an average of forty-six dollars. Never had got that much for an animal in my life. I was so tickled, I jest had to buy somethin'. My customer told me about the Collins Brothers' shop, so I went on over there, and bought this saddle off the rack. Paid in gold coin, too. Cost near as much as a steer, but it was for sure worth that and more."

He pointed to the saddle. "That's Sam Stagg riggin', and you'll never see it on anythin' but a slick fork. I had the wool pad taken off, when sheepskin came into use, about four years ago. Other than that, nothin's been changed. I never rode a better, more comfortable saddle...."

I led the bay out, and stepped aboard. He never so much as flicked an ear. Judah reined past me, headed toward the ranch gate, and the bay followed in a fast, shuffling single-foot. A whiskey-filled glass would have balanced on my head. I felt at home on the horse, and it was obvious I'd ridden a lot of horseback miles.

We rode along for three or four miles, with Judah pointing out landmarks and boundaries and explaining them. Then we came to the Dodge road, and he reined up abruptly, swearing under his breath.

Coming toward us, away from Dodge, was a rib-sprung mare dragging a blanket-wrapped figure on a travois. At the animal's head was a skinny Indian woman dressed in filthy old buckskin clothing, her feet wrapped in blanket remnants. In her left hand she carried an ancient flintlock musket, with the barrel sawed off short and brass tacks on the stock.

She looked up as her sorry outfit came abreast of us. A muttered warning came from the figure on the travois, and a look of abject terror appeared on her face. She moaned, piteously, and tried to run, dragging the horse, which promptly balked. Screaming, she beat on the poor animal with the musket, a gibberish of Indian words spilling from her mouth. I nudged the bay with spurs, meaning to help her if I could.

Clayton reached out and grabbed my bridle.

"Jest leave her be," he said. "It's none of your affair. We'd best be on our way to Dodge." Suiting the action to the words, he kicked his horse into a lope, and I followed along. Looking back, I saw the woman standing there, shrieking curses after us. Then she began to cry....

We rode along in silence for some time. Naturally, I was curious, but I figured he would tell me what had caused that woman to be so frightened, if he felt I needed to know. The road dipped down and we forded a trickle of water in an almost dry creek bed. Off to one side was a clump of willows, where Clayton stopped and let his horse drink.

He poured a trickle of tobacco into the paper, and handed me the makin's. Clearing his throat noisily, he licked the edge of the paper, and twisted it into a cigarette. Waiting until I had completed mine, he struck a light for us both.

"Reckon you wondered what that was all about, back there," he said. "Well, it's a long story, but I'll try to make this tellin' as short as possible.

"Back in sixty-one, Nancy's mother and I were married. We had known each other all of our lives; matter of fact, were even related. Third cousins, twice removed, or somethin' close to that." He puffed on the cigarette, and then continued....

"Wasn't a month later, and the War broke out. I'd joined up in a local militia group some time before, like the rest of my friends, and we went right away.

I managed to keep my hide intact, until it ended. Stayed with Mitchell's Second, untouched, through Wilson's Creek, Perryville, and all the rest of them places. Some, I don't even remember anymore.

"They let me come home on leave in May of sixty-three, and Nancy was born nine months later. I remember May was the month I heard old Stonewall Jackson had died. Shot accidentally, by a bunch of his own Johnny Reb pickets. We felt mighty bad.

"I got home in May, two years later, and we were happy as two young kids again. Old Bud Larkin had stayed on, and had the place runnin' like a clock. He'd sold lots of beef durin' the War. Got good prices from the Army, so I had money in my bank account. Money to invest in good livestock."

He turned, and peered at me from under his hat brim. "You were out back, this mornin', and saw her grave and the skulls around it. They're all Injuns, but one." He stopped a moment or so, and then went on with his narrative....

"It was almost eighteen years ago, like the marker shows. Elizabeth was carryin' another child, and we hoped we'd have a son. She only had a month or so to go, when it happened.

"There was a cattlemen's meetin' in Kansas City. We were havin' problems with the herds comin' from Texas. Ticks covered the cattle comin' in, and our critters had no protection from the fever they carried. Bud was with me at that meetin', so my wife was at the ranch by herself. All the hands had to stay out with the herds and doctor the sick cows as best they could.

"It was a small party of Kiowas, led by a renegade white man. Like the scum that rode with Quantrill and Bloody Bill Anderson, he was meaner and more vicious than any Injun ever hoped to be.

"Me'n old Bud rode in, jest hours after they'd

been there, done their filthy work, and left headin'
north. We found my Elizabeth in that clearin', where
she's buried. They'd staked her out on the ground,
naked, and...and used her. Then, they cut her belly
open, and taken the baby out. Dashed its brains out
against a tree. It was a little boy....

"Reckon I went plumb out of my head, for a while.
Bud, he did what had to be done. I couldn't bring
myself to so much as touch her, or the child."

He began to roll another cigarette, and his hands
trembled, spilling some of the tobacco. I shook my
head when he offered the sack. Passing his sleeve
across his eyes with a rubbing motion, he continued....

"Bud found little Nancy in the barn loft. She'd
tunneled into the hay, and I thank God them devils
didn't set fire to any of the buildings. They were in
a hurry, I reckon. They had wiped out a whole family of ranchers down on the Cimarron River, and
neighbors were hot on their trail." He lit up the
cigarette, and his hands were steady again.

"Like I was sayin', I went sorta crazy for a time.
Taken a fresh horse, and lit out after them. Bud tried
to stop me, but I jest wouldn't listen. He had to stay,
on account of my Nancy. Couldn't bring her with
him, and couldn't leave her. So he taken her on out
to the cow camp, and left her with my cook. That
put him about five hours behind me and my sworn
pledge to git even with those murderous sons, no
matter what. He knew I'd kill my horse, if necessary,
so he ran in four of our best saddle horses and packed
along supplies for more'n a week.

"Well, I caught up with 'em the second night.
They'd had to stop and rest their horses. Made camp
back in a bend of the Pawnee River, and I reckon
they felt safe enough, 'cause they had a fire goin',
and meat on a spit.

"Just had one guard out; a young Injun kid. I taken care of him with my knife. The rest, and there were four of 'em, were all hunkered up to that fire. I jest naturally cut down on 'em with my double gun, bein' careful not to kill 'em all. I didn't want 'em to git off that easy, after what they done to my Elizabeth, and our boy baby."

By now, Judah had a wild look to him, and was breathing a bit heavily. I began to feel uncomfortable, listening to my new friend pouring out his grisly tale.

"Are you certain that you want to continue now, Judah?" I asked him. "No reason for you to have to relive all of this over again. Some things are better buried, like those heads perhaps should be."

"Yes," he replied. "I've never really told it all. Even Bud's never heard the whole story, though I reckon he can put two and two together, easy enough. I'm not sure why I'm tellin' you, but I'd feel better, jest gettin' it off my chest. I hope you won't mind. There's not much more to tell."

I shook my head, and told him I'd be glad to listen.

"One of them buzzards was dead, but two of the Injuns, and the white skunk, were jest wounded. I gathered up all of the guns and tied the Injuns to trees. One of 'em was wearin' a woman's bonnet, and I recognized it as Elizabeth's. The other had on her blue dress, and it had bloody hand prints all over it! I jest gutted 'em both and let them sit there, with all their innards in their laps. They kept alive for a long time. Long enough for them to watch, whilst I taken my time killin' that white animal, who was leadin' them.

"Him, I lashed between two trees. I taken special care to pick out two lively willows. Ones that were strong, but had some give to 'em. I bent down the

tops and strung him up between 'em, so's his feet
were off the ground. He had scalped my wife, but
the hair wasn't from her head. He'd strung that des-
picable trophy on a thong, and had it around his
neck.

"He started out tellin' me I'd best let him go, or
I'd be certain sorry for it. He had friends, who'd
track me down to the ends of the earth, jest to git
even. Then I started skinnin' him, and he changed
his tune a mite. Begged me to stop! Screamed and
hollered, until one of the Injuns got to cussin' him.
Then he begged me to kill him, and I figgered that
I'd had enough. He was makin' mewlin' sounds, like
some kind of animal, by then, and I was disgusted.
Mostly disgusted with myself, and what I was doin'.

"Before Bud caught up with me, I'd finished them
off with my six-gun. I cut off the heads and put them
in a grain bag, then piled the bodies next to a cut
bank and caved the dirt over them."

Listening intently, I felt somewhat repelled by
what this man's grief had forced him to do. Yet I
could understand a terrible tragedy, such as he had
faced, driving him to where he had to get his revenge in this way.

"Two questions," I told him. "First, why did you
cut off their heads? Second, you've described only
five killings. I counted nine skulls around the grave,
and one seemed to have been there only a short
time. Oh! One more question. That Indian woman;
why was she so frightened of you?"

Clayton studied my face for a moment. His hand
fumbled a bit for the tobacco in his shirt pocket,
then he spoke....

"I'm not sure now, why I taken the heads. Mebbe
I wanted some kind of a symbol to place around her
grave. I'm not at all sure about that, but I didn't stop

with just those five. Over the years, I've managed to kill at least eight more. I stalked three of those. The others I killed within range of their villages.

"It's been like some kind of thing I'm forced to do. I'd git to thinkin' about my Elizabeth, and how she looked, when we found her like that. Then I jest had to find me an Injun and kill him. Oh! I always gave 'em a fair chance. I made sure they had jest as much chance to kill me. They were all fair fights, and after some, I didn't take the head.

"I thought I had this thing licked, until about six months ago. I hadn't been prowlin' for almost two years. Then the Kiowas hit a stage over west of here. Killed three men, and a young woman, travelin' to join her husband at one of those Army posts.

"The bodies were brought in to Dodge. The woman was wearin' a blue dress, just like Elizabeth's. That night, I went out lookin' for some Injuns to kill. I got one, and that's the fresh skull you saw.

"As for that squaw being afraid of me... These goin's on didn't happen without the Injuns knowin' who was doin' them killin's. They made up a name for me. *Gui-badai!* It means Appearing Wolf, in Kiowa. They scare their kids with stories of the man-wolf, who appears only to kill."

This time his fingers didn't fumble at the pocket. Deftly he rolled the cigarette, and got it going with a match. I didn't know what to say, but apparently nothing was needed. He stuck out his hand and I took it. We sat there a moment, his gray eyes boring into mine. His grip was firm and warm, and I knew that whatever he had done, it was justified by an experience so terrible it could have broken most men.

Pinching out his cigarette, he reined his horse around in a half circle, stood tall in the stirrups for a moment, then settled back in the saddle.

"C'mon, Case. Dodge is more'n four miles yet. We'd best git goin' and do our errands, or we'll never git back to the ranch in time for supper."

CHAPTER THREE

DESPITE THE SLIGHT headache remaining from my accident, I felt very good. The clean, fresh air of these rolling plains was like a tonic. I sucked in a chestful, and tasted the warm fragrance of sun on grass. It was a wonderful feeling! Just being alive, though I knew nothing about my past, or my plans for the future. Just being alive was enough!

High in the sky above us, three large birds soared in endless, sweeping circles. White on the trailing edge of their wings marked them as turkey buzzards. I felt a slight chill, though the sun was warm on my shoulders. It was great being alive, but Death was always there, waiting....

Lost in my thoughts, I was suddenly aware that Judah had asked me a question.

"I'm sorry," I said. "Mind was a million miles away. If you'd repeat that, I'd be obliged."

"I jest asked how you liked that bed last night. Was the mattress as comfortable as it looks to be? Nancy put everything together that you see in that room. The furniture we built out of walnut. A tree that must have been a couple of hundred years old

25

fell down in a big windstorm, and I sawed it into planks. Stored it in the barn loft for ten years or more. You must have noticed the beautiful grain.

"Anyways, about three years back, Nancy decided to put together the things she'd like to have, when she married. I'd intended that room for my son, but I told her to go on ahead and use it, however she liked. I helped with some things.

"You're the first person to ever sleep in the bed, or use that room, for that matter. I'm glad we had a place handy."

I felt uncomfortable about imposing on his hospitality to any further degree, and told him so. "Look, Judah," I said. "Don't think for a moment that I'm not grateful, because I am. But I can't just turn into some kind of a star boarder. Better if I find myself a place in Dodge. I'll make out all right, believe me."

He snorted, and jerked his head, impatiently. "Huh! What makes you think you'd be stayin' for free? Lotta chores got to be done around a place. Cowhands are funny critters. If they can't git somethin' done from the back of a horse, they jest won't do it!

"If you're any hand with a hammer and saw, you'll earn my thanks, plus thirty and found. How's that sound? I been to the big stockyards in KayCee, and watched the vets doctorin' calves in a squeezer chute. Had a feller draw me a picture. Shows jest how it can be made, but it takes more'n two hands to put it together. What do you say? Will you help me out? Meanwhile, you can git some decent grub, and mebbe you'll be able to git back your memory. No harm to try, anyways."

I laughed. "You win, Judah! Don't reckon I'd get myself much of a place with the few dollars in my pocket, and without any prospects of a job."

We continued on toward Dodge at an easy lope, with Judah pointing out places along the way. Topping a rise, we looked downslope at the sprawling cluster of cabins, houses, and places of business called Dodge City. It was more, far more, than I had anticipated seeing in the middle of the plains.

Judah read my thoughts. "Growin' bigger every day. Over two thousand folks livin' here now. Two years ago, mebbe a thousand two hundred could be counted as permanent; ten years back, about all you'd see was greasy buffalo hunters, and dirty bullwhackers."

He pointed towards a tall building near the edge of town, and to the right of the military road we were traveling.

"That'll be our first stop. The Ford County Courthouse. Bill Tilghman's office and jail are on the lower floor."

A lot of wagon traffic was on the road, mostly headed to the west, toward town. One, a high-sided affair with the tailboard dangling, held a pair of children of perhaps six or seven. The boy, showing a gap-toothed grin, waved at us enthusiastically. The little girl kept her eyes cast down. As we passed, I read the letters painted on the canvas four feet high— HEADED HOME.

Nearing the edge of town, a skinny old man in a mud-caked buckboard hollered at Judah and pointed toward the side of the road. Sawing at the lines, he turned off and stopped.

We waited for another wagon to pass, then crossed over to the far side and joined the oldster.

"Howdy, Rufe." Judah greeted him friendly enough, though I could sense he wasn't all that pleased.

"This here's a friend of mine. Name's Case. Case, Rufus Shelby. Rufus has a place north of us a few

miles. Come in here about the same time as me.
What's on your mind, Rufe?"

The old man was sizing me up out of watery,
squinted eyes. "What happened to yore head?" he
asked me. "Injuns skulp yuh, or somethin'? Don't
recollect seein' yuh around these parts. Stranger,
ain't yuh!" His thin nose twitched, wiggling long
hairs of a sparse mustache, and making his resemblance to an old pack rat very real.

Judah spoke up before I could form a reply.

"What did you want, Rufe? We're sort of in a
hurry. Got to speak with the Marshal."

Shelby's face flushed, and his eyes glittered.
"Don't want nothin'," he bit out. "Luke Short's in
town. Got in yesterday from Fort Worth. Talk around
town is he's on the prod."

"So?" asked Judah. "What's that got to do with
me? The bunch he's sore at ain't particular friends
of mine."

"Tom Nixon's yore friend, ain't he, and he was
thick with Deger and Bond, when Deger was mayor.
Far as thet goes, the new marshal's practically a
relative, and Luke's never cared much fer Bill Tilghman."

"What's this about Bill bein' practically a relative?" A flush was beginning to show on Judah's
face, and his jaw was knotted below his ear.

Shelby drew back. "Sparkin' yore Nancy, ain't
he? Seems he's always out to yore place anymore,
'stead of tendin' the law here in Dodge. See here,
Judah, you ain't got no reason to git all flustered
with me. I was jest tryin' to keep you out of trouble.
You know yuh don't stand a chance agin' the likes
of Luke Short. He's a killer! Killed a feller jest a few
years back, for no reason at all. Down in Arizona,
that was. Got out of it scot-free, with a slap on the

wrist. We wouldn't want to see thet happen to you, Judah."

"Yeah. Well, thanks, Rufe. See you around." He glanced at me and gigged his horse into a lope. I followed, and we left a startled old man sitting all by himself.

"What was all that about?" I asked him. "Do you expect a problem with this fellow, Short?"

He looked at me wryly, and laughed out loud....

"You weren't takin' that old coot serious, were you? Why, he's like that old hen in the nursery rhymes. Always cryin' wolf, and for no good reason. Luke Short's not a bad feller at all. Had his differences with the city fathers some time back, but that's all straightened out now. Leastways, it is as far as I'm concerned. Luke and me ain't exactly the best of friends, but we certainly ain't enemies."

We rounded a corner and loped on toward the courthouse, in actuality a three-story building. Built on a slope, with two full stories raised above the highest point, its lowest section housed the jail and marshal's office; the entry from the rear. A young man was just leaving as we drew up, with an angry look on his face. He jerked his reins loose from a metal hitchrack, and left in a shower of gravel.

"Wonder what that was all about," I mused aloud....

Judah just shrugged and motioned me up to the door, left open by the last visitor. We walked in and found Tilghman, a cigar in his teeth, elbow-deep in paperwork.

He grinned up at us, and motioned toward the mess on his desk.

"The last feller wasn't all that neat in his book-keeping," he told us. "I ain't the worlds best, but this is awful! I got tax notices here that belong to the sheriff's office; a bunch of reward dodgers, most of 'em for fellers known to be dead for years; and unpaid bills for supplies and prisoners' food that the city should have taken care of last year. It sure beats me what he did with his time. He wasn't exactly noted for his arrest record."

"Did you get an answer from the Colt Company?" I asked.

"Don't know," he replied. "Let's go on over and ask the telegrapher. It's just over in the next block." He reached up and grabbed his hat and gunbelt off the rack. Standing, he started to strap on the fancy holster rig.

I reached out a hand. "May I?'" I asked. "Don't remember ever seeing an outfit quite like that one...." Confused, I dropped the outstretched hand and started to stammer....

"What am I saying? I don't remember anything.... Not one damn thing! I ... I don't even know my own name!"

"Hey! Take it easy, old son." Tilghman's tone was soothing and gentle. "What you asked just now...Could be a sign you are beginning to remember more of your past. Here! Take all of the time you want." He handed over the belt and holstered revolver.

Near new, the belt and holster were beautifully carved in an intricate design of leaves and vines. In addition to the normal loops holding the pouch to the back plate, the toe of the pouch rested in a socket of leather at the bottom of the plate. I seemed to be familiar with normal design, and recognized this as something different.

The revolver was a single-action Colt, in .44–40 caliber, and _Frontier Six Shooter_ was etched on the left side of its barrel. Nickle-plated, it bore beautiful pearl stocks, and *Wm. M. Tilghman* was engraved on the backstrap. It was a beautiful, well-balanced weapon, and I said as much as I handed it back to the owner.

He nodded in agreement. "Yeah! Hank Garis gave that gun to me. We were partners in the Crystal Palace saloon, a few years back, and he gave it to me as a sort of a parting gift, the day we sold the business. I had the holster rig made up by a new saddle maker in Kansas City. Shipley's his name, a real artist with leather. Charles P. Shipley. He said that I was his first cash customer, and he wanted to make it real special. Reckon he did, 'cause I've never seen better. The saddle I ordered, and paid for, should be rollin' in any day now." He buckled up the belt and put on his hat....

"Well! Let's go and find out who you are, stranger."

"Who was that young'un that went scootin' out of here, in such an all-fired hurry?" It was Judah asking the question. "He like to tore the hitchrail down, gittin' his reins off. Shore looked like he was awful mad about something."

"That was young Dickerson," replied Bill. "He's been after me to make him a deputy. I've told him it was up to the City Council. That I don't have the say-so, but he just will not listen. 'Fraid I made a mistake in tellin' him he's too young for the job, and to wait a couple of years or so."

Leading our horses, we walked over to the next street, as Tilghman and Judah spoke about some plans they had made. My mind was a million miles away, as the thoughts of what might be waiting at the telegraph office whirled through my head.

Those scars I'd found on my body...Maybe my true identity would prove to be unwelcome. I might even be a criminal, a wanted man! And here I was, walking down the road with my friend, the marshal. What choice would he have but to lock me up? I shook my head vigorously, trying to chase the wild thoughts from my mind.

"What's the matter, Case?" Judah asked me. "Got a bee in your ear, or somethin'?"

"No! It's nothing like that, Judah. I'm just nervous, I guess. What a fix to be in! Not even knowing who I am!"

We had turned the corner, and Tilghman pointed at a building halfway up the block. A large sign above the doorway read U.S. SIGNAL SERVICE OFFICE. Tilghman led the way inside.

The clerk, a thin-faced older man with a very prominent Adam's apple, looked up from a stack of forms. His eyes lit up as he recognized the marshal.

"Well! Good day to you, Marshall Tilghman! I have an answer to your wire, sir. Came in less than an hour ago. This traffic has been very busy today, or I'd have run it over to you earlier." He shuffled through the forms on the counter, picked one out, and handed it to Tilghman.

The marshal scanned it quickly, frowning, then passed it over to me.

Nervously, my hand trembling, I read the message, written in a fine, Spencerian hand. It was brief....

No sales representative Colt Company in field—No sample as described issued sales personnel—signed—W.B. Franklin Vice-President and General Agent—Colt Hartford Conn.

Well, that was it.... My hopes hadn't been too high; however, slim as the chance had been, I'd still expected a clue to my identity. Some advice, perhaps, as to where I'd start looking for more information. Judah and Tilghman tried hard to cheer me up.

"C'mon," suggested Tilghman. "Let's hop over to the Long Branch, and see if Roy Drake and Frank Warren have stocked a decent brand of whiskey. Treat's on me!"

"Yeah!" agreed Judah. "They were the ones hollerin' loudest, when Short and Harris owned the place. Claimin' they'd found snakeheads, and such, in the bottles. I'm all for it. How about you, Case? A drink or two'll mebbe cheer you up."

I wasn't much in the mood, but I agreed to go along. The saloons and most of the business places were located along Front Street, just a couple of blocks over.

As we rode along, both Tilghman and Judah exchanged words with passing pedestrians and horsebackers. They seemed more or less friendly with everyone. Several looked curiously at my bandaged head but didn't venture any questions. Since I couldn't fit my hat over the bulky bandage, I'd left it back at Judah's ranch. Made me feel self-conscious, but there wasn't much I could do about that.

Ahead of us, a huge wooden replica of a rifle bulked far over the street. At least ten feet in length, it formed a sign for the F.C. Zimmerman hardware store. A portly man—Mr. Zimmerman no doubt—was standing in front as we drew up in response to Tilghman's waving arm.

Remaining on his horse, the marshal greeted him, then introduced me to the store owner.

"Zimmerman here has about the most complete gun inventory in Kansas. Knows 'em all. Could be he can help us out with your problem. Describe that leather case of yours."

I reached down and shook Zimmerman's proffered hand. In describing the contents of the case,

I referred to the long-barreled .38 as a "Cop and Thug" model. That brought a quick response from the gun dealer.

"That might be a clue," he told us. "Colt calls that gun a New Model Police Pistol in their catalog, but there's some outfit in Chicago put that name on it. I've got some of the broadsides they sent out. Let me take a look inside. Might not be a bad idea for you to come along. Maybe you will see something else that'll help."

His store was well laid out. A counter across the front held a large brass cash register, and small models of wood-burning stoves. Glass-fronted cases displayed handguns, all the popular makes; while a long rack across the back had a variety of rifles and shotguns. In one corner, I could make out the outline of a bench covered with tools, and guns all in parts. A foot-powered lathe and drill press stood close by, with plenty of steel shavings scattered about. This man kept mighty busy, that was plain to see.

Rummaging through a pile of papers on his cluttered desk, Zimmerman selected three placards. He gave them to me with an admonition.

"Pay no attention to the prices there. That's my cost at wholesale prices." He smiled, ruefully. "There's not a big profit in selling the new guns. I make more in repairs, and fine-tuning the belt guns. You see what I mean there, about the name, Cop and Thug?"

Looking them over, I saw the name, Hibbard, Spencer, Bartlett Company—Chicago, across the top of each broadside. A list of the items offered for sale covered the page. Toward the bottom of the sheets was the revolver we made reference to; the long-barreled .38, with the figures of an officer and a derbied thug molded in the gutta percha grips. The words *Cop & Thug* appeared beneath, together with a glowing account of the efficiency and reliability of the weapon.

"That's the only outfit I've ever heard refer to that gun as you did," said Zimmerman. "Course you might've seen this broadside somewheres else, but I got me a hunch you're working for them. Anyways, sit down and write them a letter. I got a suspicion you'll find out who, and what, you are.

"Oh! By the way," he added. "If you decide to sell them guns, give me first chance at 'em, will you? I'd give you a good price for 'em, and it'd be cash money."

Judah stuck his head in the doorway, a half-filled mug of beer in his hand.

"C'mon up the street, when you're done talkin' there. We got thirsty and went on over to the Long Branch. Horses're tied out in front, yours included. Take your time."

"Hold on," I told him. "I'm all through here." Turning, I thanked Zimmerman for his efforts.

"As for the guns," I said. "I don't think they are mine, but if they were, I'd hang on to them. Thanks anyway. I'll see you again, Mr. Zimmerman."

He smiled, and waved me out of the store. "Don't forget, I get first crack, if you decide to sell those guns."

The Long Branch was just four doors down the street. Now that I had another clue to follow, I somehow felt better; at any rate, better enough to be looking forward to a cold beer.

Judah stood aside, and waved me through the front door. I blinked as my eyes tried to focus in the dimly lit room. A shoulder slammed into my chest, knocking me off balance, and into Judah, who was just behind me. My spurs tangled and I fell hard, cracking my head on the boardwalk outside.

"What the hell..." hollered Judah.

A bitter taste filled my mouth, and the pain bit deep, like a hot brand searing my skull. I shook my head for a moment and looked up at a burly man framed in the doorway. A thick black beard covered most of his face, and his bloodshot eyes were glaring at me, malevolently.

"Maybe that'll teach yuh to stay out of a man's way, when he's in a hurry," he said thickly, slurring his words, as a man in his cups will do. Stepping from the doorway, he aimed a deliberate kick toward my side.

Enraged, I grabbed at his pant leg and jerked him down on the walk beside me.

"Now, we're on the same level!" I rasped, and slammed the heel of my palm into his unprotected face. I felt the bones crumple in his nose. As he raised both hands to his face, I smashed a fist into his stomach, driving out the wind with a gush of whiskey-laden breath; then again, in the same place.

He rolled over on his side, and his legs drew up, protectively. Not satisfied, I drew back for a shot at his exposed jaw, but a hand caught my fist in an iron grasp.

"He's had enough, Case. Calm down; he's had all he needs today." It was Judah, and he helped me to my feet, where we stood for a moment, my head still spinning.

I looked up and straight into the eyes of Bill Tilghman. He had a strange look on his face, a puzzled look. Then his face cleared, and he reached out a hand.

"Let's go inside and have that drink I promised. Things like that're happenin' 'round here all the time. Don't worry about that drunk. He won't even remember you, when he wakes up. Some fellers just go on the prod, when they git a belly full of likker."

The buzzing in my head had stopped, and aside from an accelerated heartbeat, I felt fine. I said as much.

They both laughed, and Judah clapped his big hand hard on my back.

"Shore don't pay to scratch this feller's itch, when he's got it. I'd sooner be bedded down with a full-growed grizzly bear, nursin' a mouthful of sore teeth."

"Yep," Tilghman replied. "He didn't want to quit, either. Good thing you grabbed his hand. That feller was about done in, what with the likker, and Case here bustin' his nose, an' punchin' clean through to his backbone."

A couple of spectators stepped aside and let us in to the saloon. The bar, a carved and ornate affair, stood against the far wall, its white-painted front gleaming in the light from the numerous hanging chandeliers. The mirrored backbar had a huge pair of steer horns mounted above, and was adorned with Indian trophies. Bows and arrows, feathered war bonnets, shields, and drums hung from nails.

The bartender, a pleasant-faced younger man, took a swipe with his rag and set out a bottle and three glasses.

"Doc, here, is buyin'." He motioned toward a middle-aged man standing near the far end of the bar. "He'd have taken that feller on hisself, but he ain't no prize ring fighter."

"Yes!" The older man stepped forward. "Let me shake the hand that punched that bully silly. If I had been armed, I'd have put a bullet into him!"

His grasp was strong, though his hand was very small. We looked each other over and I liked what I saw. Most of his face was concealed behind a huge mustache and Van Dyke beard, but his clear blue eyes bespoke honesty and forthrightness. Right now, his expression was open, and one of admiration.

"Good job, young man. Well done, I must say. I'm Thomas McCarty. I have the local drugstore, and I am a practicing physician here in Dodge City. I'm usually the one who binds up the wounds around here, but I see someone has done a very professional job on you, already. Whatever happened to your head, my boy? Is it a recent wound you have there?"

I explained how Judah had found me next to the tracks in a dazed condition, and how his daughter, Nancy, had stitched up the lacerations and bandaged my noggin.

"Well, I'll know where to send my surplus patients in the future. Nancy's a fine girl! I'm surprised that one of our young men hasn't already taken advantage of her eligibility. In my day..."

Judah laughed. "Ain't up to them, Doc. Nancy's got certain ideas about what sorta feller she'll spend the rest of her natural-borned life with. She's very levelheaded."

Tilghman nodded. "You can bet your last cartwheel on it. Nancy and I are just friends, of course, but she has confided in me in some of our conversations. Believe me, whatever young man puts a ring on her finger better have both of his feet planted solidly on the ground."

I noticed that he had turned his glass upside down while the bartender began to pour, and held up his hand, palm out. As the rest of us raised our glasses in a toast, I commented on his forbearance.

"Are you passing the drink because you're on duty, Bill? I'm sure that no citizen of Dodge would begrudge their duly elected marshal one potion. It seems to be a regular occurence for the rest of the populace."

"No! I've been known to take a sip on occasion, but most of the time I try to stay away from likker and tobacco. Aim to live a long and productive life, myself, and I figger the less I punish this body of mine, the better chance I got."

"Here, here!" cried McCarty. "I'll drink to that!"

"There," added Judah. "We got the word of a medical man. That makes it 'most the same as a prescription. I'll buy us all another round, then Case and I gotta git goin'. Samuel! Pour us another drink, if you will." He dug down in a pocket and produced a coin.

After draining our glasses, we shook hands all around. I thanked Tilghman again for sending the wire to the Colt Company.

"Do I owe you anything for the telegram, Bill? I haven't got a whole lot of money right now, but I'll have wages coming from Judah in a month or so."

He shook his head, and didn't show surprise at the fact I was going to work for Judah Clayton.

"No, Case. That's a government service, and I rated that telegram as official business. Good luck on your new job. I had considered offering you a place with me, as an assistant deputy. You've certainly proved that you can handle people. Even when you're at a disadvantage. We could talk about it, when you finish up the job with Judah. The pay's a hundred, but you'd have to find living quarters in town. You fellers hang on to your topknots, y'hear?"

Outside, the bearded man was gone. My feelings were really those of relief. During the scuffle, I had let myself get carried away, but now I had no desire for further fighting. I wondered about that. Apparently, I had the ability to take care of myself. What had occurred must have been my true nature asserting itself. Yet I felt that under ordinary circumstances, I wouldn't seek out trouble. I hoped not, anyway.

We spent the next hour at Wright & Beverly's

store, picking out the hardware we'd need for Judah's squeezer chute, a contraption that Bob Wright seemed to know a lot about. The sun was lowering in the sky as we left the building, and we wasted no time straddling our horses and heading for home.

CHAPTER FOUR

WITH EACH PASSING day, I became more appreciative of that extreme good fortune which had deposited me on the Clayton's doorstep, so to speak. Also, more at peace with myself and my elusive memory.

The hard work, the fine, wholesome meals, and the blessed nights of dreamless sleep...All combined to make me feel a new man.

Somehow, I sensed that my life had not been this free and easy in the past. Especially the nights. It was nothing I could explain. Just a feeling that crept into my thoughts.

Judah and I had completed the squeezer chute, and experimented with a few late calves that had escaped ear notching and, in the case of the bull calves, castration. It worked!

The animals were released from the corral, and ran down a narrow passage of posts and rails. At the end, where they'd seen blue sky and freedom, was the squeezer. I stood on top of the contraption, holding a long lever which was connected to one side of the last section of fence; a side that was hinged at the bottom, so it could be swung over against whatever animal we were handling, pinning it solidly between the two sides. A series of dogs, or catches, held it in place until we were finished. Then, it was a simple matter to release the dogs and let the animal go free.

It was so easy to operate, and much safer than roping and throwing the calves. Plus, as Judah had explained, it took four men and a horse to rope, throw, hold, and treat the calves. I wondered why he hadn't thought to install a chute some time before. His answer had been laconic....

"Well...I only put my pants on one leg at a time. The buildin' of this ranch has taken me most of my workin' life. More'n likely there's other gadgets that'd save time, but we jest ain't come across 'em yet, I reckon."

The month of May was almost run out, and the past weeks I had spent on the ranch seemed more like days. My head healed quickly, and the bandage was no longer required; plus the hair was gradually covering the scars. If my physical condition had been good when I arrived, it was even better now.

I had taken to wearing a six-gun, at the insistence of the foreman, Bud Larkin. Judah agreed, and gave me the lend of a nice, worn old holster rig he'd had for years.

"Got that from the Collins Brothers," he told me. "Time I was in Omaha, and bought that saddle you're usin'. I had me a long-barreled forty-five Colt. Still got it, but never carry the old relic anymore. Guess it could be put back in shape, but it'd likely cost more'n it's worth. Cylinder stops are wore clean out, and it won't lock up anymore; so that means a new cylinder, and mebbe some inside parts.

"Bought it mail-order back in seventy-six from J.P. Moore and Sons, in New York. It was an Army reject, and it's marked U.S. on the frame. I couldn't see a damn thing wrong with it. Them government inspectors is persnickety, I reckon. Worry about polishing, and so forth. Main thing was, it shot jest fine, and the price was sure right. Paid thirteen dollars, plus freight.

"This holster caught my eye, and I liked it fine, but the barrel of my gun was too long. Taken me a minute to figger out the cure for that. Gunsmith down the street cut it off, and reset the sight. Like Tilghman said the other day, the short barrels is easier to git out, when you need 'em fast.

"Now, I ain't layin' no claim to bein' a gunslick, but we live in difficult times, and it pays a man to be ready, when and if trouble does come. You pay attention to old Bud, and you keep a gun handy. We done enough patchin' on you, up to now, and I don't want the job of buryin' you, or anyone else. You wear this rig, wherever you ride."

Judah and I were of a size, so the belt fit perfectly. I checked the belt loops, and found they would hold .44s, even though they had been sewn for the larger cartridges. Of the six-guns in the case, I had already chosen the short-barreled .44 Frontier as my idea of a belt gun. Lighter, of course, if for no other reason, and I liked the balance.

One of the ranch hands had been jumped by a half dozen of the young reservation bucks out scouting for easy pickings. They'd chased him halfway to headquarters, but they ran off when he decided to make a stand with his saddle gun instead of riding a good horse to death.

As Bud had pointed out, he'd been lucky. If he hadn't been on his horse with his carbine in the boot, they'd have gotten him for sure. Dismounted, and treating a roped calf, he would have been defenseless.

Temporarily, Judah and I had run out of work around home, so at breakfast he assigned me to ride fence with a young puncher named Fannin, Buck Fannin.

As I waited for Buck to complete some last-minute chore, I got to looking over Rusty, the blood-bay gelding that I'd been using steadily since I'd first shown up at the ranch. Despite the sunny day and my feeling of well-being, a wave of despondency crept over me.

Everything was borrowed. The horse, the saddle, bridle, rope, chaps.... Even the clothes I was standing in, from the skin on out. They all belonged to Judah. I had nothing of my own, not even my real name! How much longer would I have to go, before I'd be a whole man again?

Fannin's arrival, on a big, feisty buckskin, meant an end to my black thoughts. It was hard to feel blue with a grinning, freckled youngster like Buck around. As I watched, he deliberately gigged that buckskin in a tender spot....

"Heyyy Yahhh!" he hollered, as the outraged gelding reared skyward, plunged down on stiffened legs, hopped, and threw his hind feet even higher. Buck raked him again, and with a third stiff-legged plunge from the horse, he went sailing over the horse's head and fell rolling in the dirt.

The buckskin trotted off, his head held to one side so's not to step on the trailing reins. I jumped up on Rusty, my rope building into a loop, and ran the horse down. Bringing him back, I handed the reins to Buck.

"Thanks, Case," the youngster panted, brushing manure and dirt off the seat of his britches. "Reckon you're wonderin' why I did that?"

I grunted.

"Wellsir. When I first come here to work, my name

was an old family one. Michael Aloysius Fannin. Now, there was already two fellers here named Mike, and I'd fight before I'd answer to Aloysius, so they decided to call me Three.

"That is, until I picked out my string, and this here old buckskin was the easiest of the bunch to ride. Well, we got out with the cows, and he caught me half asleep, and promptly went to buckin'. I landed on my head, and he jest stayed there lookin' at me.

"From that time, he'd be gentle as a kitten, until the right moment. Then he'd dump me, purty as you please. Fellers got to callin' me Buck, 'cause of the buckin' buckskin, I reckon. Now I got me this little scheme worked out. I make sure all the buckin' gits done right at the beginnin', so's I can be sure of this horse, when I need him most."

I shook my head. "Whatever you say, Buck. But seems the horse is getting the better of the deal. Why don't you just try and break him of the habit?"

He looked at me, like I didn't have good sense. Swinging up into the saddle, he chose his words deliberately....

"Look, Case. I ain't gonna ride no horse that ain't even got a little bit of spirit. Don't want no rockin' horse. I look good, when the horse looks good. That is, if I stay on the durned thing. C'mon, we got a lot of ridin' to do!"

Heading almost due north, we reached the first stretch of fence in about an hour. I don't know what I expected to see, but I wasn't prepared for the thick, impenetrable hedges almost as high as my shoulder.

"Osage," Buck informed me. "We're gradually fencin' with new-fangled bobbed wire, but me, I'd jest as soon milk cows, and raise chickens, as to fool with that durn stuff. Hedges are natural. Good strong osage'll keep cows in and varmints out, and it don't git rusty. Old man Glidden was workin' in the Devil's trail sign when he invented bobbed wire."

We rode along the hedgerow at a trot, with Buck keeping a running patter of conversation going. The graze looked good to me. It was short, but there was a lot of it. The cattle we passed were fat and healthy-looking, and carrying Judah's J-C brand on their left hip. Here and there I saw where the barbed wire had been used to close an opening in the hedges. The gnarled osage branches were charred and blackened.

"Injuns," replied Buck, when I asked him. "Bucks build a fire in under the hedge, and wait for it to burn through. A feller'd have to have six sets of eyes to ketch 'em at it."

"Well, why do they do it?" I asked him. "They can't possibly burn down all of it, and what's burned grows back."

"There's your answer." He pointed up in the sky, ahead of us. Two buzzards were circling over a shallow draw.

Buck kicked the buckskin into a run, and I followed right along. A moment later, we were looking down at what remained of two fat young heifers. An arrow was buried almost to the feathers behind the shoulder of one. The other had been shot.

"Look!" he said bitterly. "All they taken was the loins and tongues." He got down and knelt over one of the cows.

He pointed out the stiffened hide, curling at the opening in the stomach cavity. "Dead close to two weeks. We worked this part of the range, just about that far back. They must have come in soon after. Damn! Two young heifers, and both carryin' calf starts too. Lookee there in that 'un. Little bones, and you can make out a skull."

He was right! It *was* a waste! From the sign left

at the carcasses, it was obvious the thieves had been on horseback. Most of that meat could have been carried away.

Buck had gotten out a small black book. Laboriously, he was scribbling on one of the pages. Looking up, he saw that I was watching, an unspoken question on my face.

"Tally book," he told me. "You oughta git yourself somethin' like this. Comes in handy, when you want to remember. S'posin' you see some cows, or a strayed horse, and they are wearin' brands you never did see before? Copy 'em down, and you can trace the owners. Me! I never can remember nothin' from one day to the next, 'ceptin' payday and mealtimes. I write down all sorts of things." He stuffed the book and a stub of pencil in his chaps pocket.

We mounted up, and continued to patrol the hedgeline. My senses were all alert. The land was rolling, and any one of dozens of draws and gullys could have hidden a dozen Indians or more. Buck must have read my mind, because he glanced at me and chuckled.

"Don't you worry none about them Injuns. They're long ago gone from around here. They know we can read the buzzard sign, jest as plain as they can. 'Nother thing; they'd pass up jumpin' two of us, less'n they was real desp'rit for powder'n ball, or cartridges. Ammunition's purty hard for them to come by these days. Army watches the traders close."

About two hours later, we came up on a small knoll. Buck reined in, and climbed down off the buckskin.

"Time for dinner," he told me. Slipping out the bit and letting it dangle beneath the horse's jaw, he drove in a pin and uncoiled his picket rope. He glanced at me from over a shoulder as he loosened both the cinches.

"What're you waitin' for, Case? Dinner time! Do you expect a written invite?"

I wasn't all that sure where "dinner" was coming from, as I hadn't seen any lunch packed, but I wasted no time in complying. A moment later I watched as he dug down in his saddle bags and brought out two cans of peaches and a slab of jerked beef.

"Here!" he told me. "Git yourself a seat, and dig in! I guess we oughta eat the beef first, 'cause peaches to me are dessert. Sorry I couldn't fetch coffee along. It'd be purty tasty, right about now, but we'd have to build a fire."

Coffee or no coffee, it surely did taste good! I wolfed down my share in no time at all and, leaning back, I accepted tobacco and papers from my providing partner.

"Wonder what the pore folks are doin' about now," he commented with a sly grin. "Don't you worry none, about Judah not wantin' us to take a break at mealtime. He's purty good about things like that. Man's gotta have his rest and grub. Makes him want to work that much harder, when there's cattle needin' help, or fences to be mended.

"Now, I'm jest gonna rear back, close my eyes, and git me 'bout fifteen minutes of shut-eye. You might do the same."

Adjusting his hat over his face, he did just that. I was too keyed up to think about sleep, so I decided to walk and do some thinking.

Ahead of me, I heard the sound of a quail calling, and in the distance an answer. Moments later, the "whirrrr" of the quail's wings as they flushed from a close brushclump just about scared the pants off me. I caught myself just in time, gun half drawn from the holster. I grinned, self-consciously. Good thing I was out here by myself. Grown man scared by a bunch of quail...

It was a real puzzle. All of this seemed to be so familiar to me. The horses, the cattle, the wild-life...And yet I couldn't remember a simple thing like my own given name.

That knock on the head. Falling, or being pushed off the train. Why would anyone want to push me? What would I have been doing out on the platform, when the train still had several miles to go before the stop in Dodge? None of it made any sense!

I decided that Buck's fifteen minutes must be about up by now, so I headed back toward the horses. Off the trail, to my right, the sun glinted off something hanging on a bush. I stepped over and found it to be a strip of deerskin covering a curious design in multicolored beads. It roughly resembled the figure of a man wearing blue pants and a red shirt. I stuffed it in my shirt pocket, guessing it to be a piece of Indian decoration of some kind.

Buck was on his feet, a cigarette hanging from his lips. He'd replaced the bit in his horse's mouth, and was tightening the cinches on his saddle.

"'Bout time you got back," he said. "Time's a-wasting. I can't do all the work around here, you know." The last was said with a grin as he pinched out the cigarette and vaulted up into the saddle.

We continued to follow the line of hedges, the sun bright in our faces as we rode westward. What cattle we found too close to the fence we bunched and ran off for a mile or so.

"You certain sure you've never done this before?" Buck's look of puzzlement was comical to see. We'd just finished a small gather, and had them moving along at a trot. One bull had made up his mind to stand his ground, and I'd made a few passes toward him, each time dodging when he had gotten me into position for a charge.

On the last one, he'd made his move; and I kneed

my horse out of his way, catching him a tremendous whack with my rope coil. He broke into a run, leading the rest in the direction that we had wanted them to go.

"Don't you try'n tell me you ain't never herded cows before, 'cause I know better!" Buck was indignant. "Man don't jest git on a horse and know what to do when an old, range-wise bull decides to stomp him in the ground. You done thet with your knees. I saw you! You never touched a rein!"

I was confused now, and didn't know what to say. I tried to explain that to the irritated young cowpuncher, who obviously thought he was being mocked.

"I'm sure it was the horse, Buck.... No... I'm not sure of anything. You have to just believe me, because I have no idea of what I've done in my past. My life... the life I'm living right now... started for me on Wednesday, May seventh."

He just stared, and then shrugged his shoulders. Gigging the buckskin, he made one last run at the cattle, and forced them into a clumsy gallop away from the hedges.

We rode along in silence for some time. I felt badly, my mind was a jumble, but there wasn't any more I could say. I felt, as he did, that what I had done out there came from my experience. It was no accident that I had known what to do at just the right moment. But try as hard as I might, that past of mine remained a closed door.

Buck's nudge jarred me out of my daydreams. We'd climbed a bench, and down below us was a patch of swampy ground. My eyes spotted the cow first, mired down in the ooze, with her head just barely showing. Then I saw her calf. Lying there motionless, trying to hide, with no cover at all.

Reacting quickly, Buck half jumped, half slid his horse's bulk down through the loose pebbles below the bench, already building a loop in his lariat. With a smooth toss, he dropped it over the cow's horns, and the buckskin leaned back into the slack, and started taking a strain.

"Back, boy. C'mon now, back up...back, back... that's it, hoss. C'mon back...."

Nothing was happening except that the cow's head was being twisted at an impossible angle. Buck looked over at me.

"What're yuh waitin' for, Case? Git a rope on her! Give me a hand here, or we're gonna lose us a cow!"

Something seemed to click in my head, and I let go of the reins, lifted a leg over the horn, and slid to the ground.

"Hold a steady strain, Buck, but don't try any harder. I got me an idea. Don't ask me why, or how I know, but if you just trust me for a moment, I'll get that cow out of there."

As I talked, I was unbuckling my chaps and loosening the gunbelt from around my waist. Sitting down, I pulled off my boots, spurs and all. Next came my pants and shirt. Though it was a warm, sunny day, gooseflesh formed on my upper body.

"What're you aimin' to do? Take you a mud bath? Purty is as purty does, and there ain't much hope for you." His tone wasn't sarcastic. More puzzled than anything else.

Grabbing my rope, I circled around behind the mired cow's vision and waded into the mud. Each step was an agony of strain, the sticky ooze clinging to my legs with a determined reluctance to let go of them.

Finally, I reached her side, and probed down through that sticky mess for a hind foot. When I had it for sure, I took the noosed end of my rope and looped it securely around her leg, just above the hoof.

Passing the rope over the cow's back, I waded laboriously around to her other side, where I repeated the procedure, in this case using a half hitch instead of a loop. Now comes the hard part, I thought to myself. Getting the cow's legs to draw up under her belly, where they'd be out of the way.

It took about all of my strength, but I got it done, and passed the taut rope around the cow's tail with a couple of half hitches. Next, I ran the rope up to a horn, brought it back to a point even with her front legs, and using another hitch to secure it, I managed to tie up her front legs, just as I'd done with those in back.

"Now!" I hollered at Buck. "Now see if she'll come out!" I twisted the cow's tail and she bellowed as the buckskin, backing up, slid her out onto dry ground. Took me only minutes to get the ropes off, and the cow lumbered to her feet. Then, with her calf following, she trotted off without even so much as a backward glance.

Buck was silent, but only for a moment. He accepted his lariat as I handed it up, and buckled it into the strap beneath his saddle horn.

"There's a creek yonder, just over that rise," he told me. "You can git all that mud washed off, so's you can git dressed in your clothes again. It ain't much of a walk, and that saddle ain't gonna be much fun to ride if you git mud smeared all over it."

Gingerly, I started to pick my way over the pebble-strewn ground, each step a "hop and skip" combination. Buck came behind, leading my horse, with all my gear piled on top. When he couldn't hold back any longer, he burst out laughing.

"Haw! Haw! Haw! I'd give me a year's pay, just

to have a feller here, like Brady, with one of them cameras. You look jest like one of them tar babies, only worst. Too bad I got no guitar. Your dancin'd be better, if you had music."

I skipped on in silence. Then I turned and grinned back at him.

"Keep it up! Soon's I get this awful stuff washed off, I figure on flinging you in that bog, clothes and all."

"Aw! I was only funnin', Case. You do look funny; still I gotta hand it to yuh. That cow slid outta that bog, slicker'n a sled on runners. Where'd yuh learn somethin' as smart as that? Now! You jest hold on there!" He was backing the buckskin, and holding out a flattened hand....

"Put that there rock down! It was a dumb question, and I take it back. I know what you're gonna say. You don't even remember a durn thing!"

"That's right," I told him. "Nothing! But I *am* about to agree with you. This is something I've done before. Where or when, I don't know. As soon as you took a strain on that rope, I knew you'd pull the legs off that cow, or at least I thought you would. The answer just popped into my head."

The water in the creek was only a few inches deep, but it was enough to wash off the clinging mud. Buck built us each a cigarette, and I puffed on that while the sun dried me. A few pats with my shirttail, and I was able to get back into my clothing.

We mounted up and spent the rest of the day chousing the cattle back from the hedges. When it finally came time, I'd had my share of riding fence for one day. We kicked both of our horses into a lope, and headed for the barn....

CHAPTER FIVE

THE SOUNDS OF a rider coming in woke me from my daydreams. Sprawled on the bunkhouse settee, I'd been plaiting a horsehair bridle, and drifted into a half-somnolent state, intent on the intricate patterns I was creating with the multicolored hairs.

A moment later, Bill Tilghman was looking down at me from the back of a beautiful blood-bay horse. Short-coupled, the chest was deep and wide, with well-defined hard muscles rippling beneath the reddish hair.

"How come you ain't in Church, 'stead of layin' there doin' the Devil's work? This is Sunday, and all the righteous folks got their hymnbooks in hand, and their backsides plunked down in a pew."

He grinned. "Got any coffee left in the bunkhouse pot? I really need somethin' to wash the dust outta my teeth."

Without waiting for an answer, he swung down and wrapped his reins around the well-worn oak hitchrail.

It being a warm day, the door was wide open, and he waved me inside with a mocking gesture. As he did so, his brocaded vest swung back, and I saw the glitter of his badge. The bar had his name, Wm. Tilghman, engraved across it, and hanging from two gold chains was a straight-sided shield, emblazoned diagonally with the title City Marshal. It was massive in its proportions, and I said as much.

He laughed. "Yeah! I call this my 'forty dollar' badge. Some of my friends had a jeweler named Durand make this from two double eagles. One thing sure. I'll never be broke, as long as I'm wearin' this badge."

I got out two cups and filled them from the pot we kept warm on the jury-rigged remnants of an old kerosene lantern. It was steaming hot, and black as tar.

Tilghman winced as he took a cautious sip. "Whew! Just how long you boys been boilin' this stuff? Careful now! If you spill this on your boots, it'll eat a hole right through 'em. I've drank lots of roundup coffee, but it'd have to go some to beat this poison!"

It was very hot in the bunkhouse, even with an open door, so we took our coffee outside and sat on the settee. I accepted a thin cigar, and we lit up from the match Bill scraped across the sole of his boot. He cleared his throat, spat, and began to speak, his eyes on my face.

"Does the name Frank Specter mean anything to you? Did you ever hear that name before? I have a reason for asking. Think carefully, now...."

I stared at him. There *was* a flicker of something in the back of my mind, but then it was gone. I tried hard, looking out across the horse corral and concentrating every effort to bring back that fleeting glimpse at something he had conjured up with that name. But it was no use, and I turned to him with a question of my own.

"Why, Bill? *Should* Frank Specter mean something to me?"

"Dunno, Case. That day in town...the day you were rollin' around on the walk with that drunk. You were purty mad, and your face was twisted up somethin' fierce. Changed your whole appearance. Didn't really look like you, at all. I'd seen that look somewheres before, but couldn't place where. Yesterday, I was goin' through some more of that mess of paperwork in the office, and I found an old copy of *Harper's Weekly*. Reckon I'd seen it somewheres else, but forgot.

"Anyways, there was a drawing of this man, Frank Specter, and a story about him. Seems he's some kind of detective or somethin'. After readin' it, I'd say he's just a hired gun. Only thing is, he's always worked on the side of the law. I brought the paper along, so's you could take a look at it."

He reached into his inside coat pocket and brought forth a thin, folded newspaper. Opening it to the second page, he folded it back and handed it to me. The sketch wasn't very clear, but there definitely was a resemblance....

What I hadn't seen in the washroom mirror were the twisted, contorted lines in the face, and the grim intensity that stared out of the eyes in the drawing.

The story was brief. It merely stated that Frank Specter was presumed dead, having disappeared from the deck of an upriver-bound Mississippi steamboat, shortly after leaving the port of St. Louis. He had been seen on an upper deck sometime after sunset, but failed to show at the supper table. A search was made of the entire vessel, but to no avail. There were no signs of a struggle, and it was assumed he'd missed his footing on the slippery deck and fallen overboard.

Specter's employers, Pinkerton National Detective Agency, had been contacted, and declined to comment. The article, a bylined piece by someone named Stone, went on to tell of an incident in which Specter had "gunned down" two men, without being harmed himself. Both had turned out to be wanted by a sheriff in Missouri for bank robbery. .

Spectators weren't sure how the encounter had begun. However, they all agreed that Specter had fired in self-defense. Inspection of the bodies showed that both men had been killed instantly, with multiple heart wounds. One had been shot three times, and the other twice. As the mortician stated, in both cases the wounds could be "covered by a four-bit piece!"

In conclusion, the writer pointed out that this was not a first-time experience for Mr. Specter. Eight men had fallen dead in front of Specter's gun, and all witnessed as shot in self-defense. This latest pair had brought his total now to ten, and testified to his ability with a handgun. His first killing had been that of a Negro soldier in 1874. The soldier's companion, another trooper, was wounded when they had attempted to catch Specter in a cross fire. The dateline on the article was in March of 1883.

I looked up at Tilghman. "Doesn't mean anything to me at all. Besides, this man Specter is apparently dead. Look! It says right here that he disappeared over a year ago. I'd certainly remember, if I was a killer like the man described in this newspaper!"

Tilghman held out a placating hand.... "Look, Case. That picture *does* resemble you. Or at least like you looked, the day you had the fracas with that drunk. I thought... Hell, I don't know what I thought! You're right! We probably all have look-alikes scattered around. Let's just forget it!"

He grinned. "Main reason I come by was to tell you about the race next Saturday. It's a footrace be-

tween a man named Sawyer, a white feller; and Bill
Hogan, a black man. The race will be three hundred
yards, for a one-thousand-dollar purse. I've been
asked to be one of the judges, and I figger I'd be
wise to have a friend or two to back me up. Never
know but what soreheads'll cause trouble, and I want
to be sure they don't take it out on me. Will you
come? Ask Judah, too. I'm sure he'd want to be
there. Matter of fact, why don't you squire Nancy
along? Give you and her a chance to get together."

I looked at him in surprise. "I'd be the last man
to try and spark your lady friend, Bill. Nancy's a fine
girl; they don't come any nicer. But I know she
wouldn't want me shining up to her, when you're
around."

Tilghman laughed.... He roared, and slapped his
thigh. I didn't see anything so darn funny about what
I'd just said.

He straightened up, tears of mirth rolling down
his face. "Don't ever let my wife hear you say that,"
he told me. "We been married for six years now,
and she won't stand for foolin' around! Nancy and
I are just friends. Her father and I been knowin'
each other for years, now. Hell! I held Nancy on my
knee when she was just a little filly, and she's told
me that I'm her favorite uncle. Nancy... Lady
friend... I never heard the beat...." He started
laughing again.

Well... I felt taken down a peg or two, but at the
same time I was elated. Nancy had never shown
more than a friendly, curious interest, but I was
definitely attracted to her. 'Course, I didn't have
much to offer a girl. Not even a name I knew to be
my own. Still...

"C'mon! What d'ya say, Case?" Tilghman had finally stopped laughing. "Can I count on you bein'
there to back me up next Saturday? There'll be plenty

of liquid refreshment, if you've a mind for that sort'a thing, and entertainment of an entirely different nature at the card tables Saturday night. Are you ... S'cuse me, Case. I reckon you do play cards. I wouldn't mind showin' you how, if you don't." He grinned at me. "You will come, won't you?"

"I don't see why not," I told him. "I'll ask Nancy, when she and Judah get back from Church. More coffee, Bill?"

"Uhh...no! Reckon I've had enough," he said. He tossed the grinds in the dirt, and handed me the empty cup. The cigar in his mouth had gone out, and he relit the stub, before climbing back on his horse. The bay was anxious to get going, and he shuffled nervously, rolling the bit in his big teeth.

"That's some kind of horse," I told Bill admiringly. "I reckon I'm not the first to tell you that. He's not really a true bay, with those two white socks, but it complements a beautiful color combination. He looks like he could run all day, so long as you kept him at a steady pace. Have you had him very long, Bill?"

That he was proud of his horse was easy to see. He took the cigar out of his mouth, and leaned down toward me.

"Used to be an Injun's horse," he told me. "Kiowa chief named White Deer owned him. Wasn't no amount of money that would tempt him into partin' with this animal. Lots of fellers tried to buy him, includin' me, but White Deer wouldn't budge. This was his 'war horse,' and part of his 'medicine,' or so he told us. I didn't offer him no guns, like some men did. Didn't want to make it any easier for him to shoot our folks than it already was. I did show him two hundred silver dollars, though, and he turned me down.

"Then a horse thief, name of Dutch Henry, turned

up mebbe two years back. Had a small band of Injun horses he'd stole in the Nations somewhere. This feller here was one of 'em.

"We talked some trade, but turned out he needed some cash money, and I gave him eighty-five dollars for Chief here. Later on, when he heard how bad I'd wanted this horse, he tried hard to buy him back. Seems folks were laughin' at him, or somethin'.

"Gotta mosey on, Case. You try and make it Saturday, you hear? Bring Nancy along, like I said. I'll see you then."

I waved as he turned the bay and headed toward Dodge. Nice feller, Bill Tilghman. I was glad that he was a friend of mine. That newspaper... Could that killer the reporter had described be me? Was it possible that I had left those ten dead men somewhere in my past? I shrugged off the doubt in my mind. If it were true, I'd have some inkling; some of the instincts of ruthlessness that drove Frank Specter. The cold-blooded insensitivity that allowed him to shoot a human being, without a care for the consequences. Gunfights could happen to any of us, here on this raw frontier. One or maybe even two or three, but ten dead men! No! Surely a man'd have to be *hunting* trouble to have been involved in so many gun duels. These were *witnessed* killings! There could perhaps be that many more that no one had seen.

Shaking my head, I tried to rid my thoughts of that paper and the ugly possibilities it offered. Deciding that a ride across the ranchland might help, I headed toward the barn.

When I brought out the saddle and bridle and racked them over the corral rails, Rusty trotted over, ready to go. I'd decided to give him a rest, however, so I dropped my loop on a rangy dun gelding that had caught my eye. Judah had let me know that any of the corraled stock was mine to ride, and I wanted to try them all.

At the last minute, I remembered to stop by the bunkhouse for my gunbelt and carbine. Also, a brush jacket, in case I stayed out after dark. The jacket I tied on behind the cantle of the saddle.

It was a grand day! The sun was high in the sky, but two or three clouds filtered the rays, and kept it from being unbearably hot. Only a few hundred yards from the barnyard, I flushed a pair of prairie chickens from a brush clump. They rose with a clatter of wings, and headed straight away, only to drop down again after a minute's flight. Judah'd told me how tame these birds had been, when he'd first settled here. Said he'd killed them with a club the first few months.

The dun wanted to run, but I held him down with a tighter than normal rein. He fidgeted for a while, but finally settled down to a steady, ground-eating lope.

It was quiet out here on the grass. The sounds of creaking saddle leather and a muffled grunt of horse breath were all I heard. I felt so free! Nothing to hold me in, as far as my eye could see. It was a great feeling! This wide and boundless prairie land was all mine to enjoy. The fragrance of the grass, crushed by the horse's feet, rose up with dust puffs that marked our passage, then settled back down to become one with the prairie sod.

I heard the *creeing* of a red-tailed hawk, and, looking up, I saw a pair in flight, soaring in great, wheeling passes in the blue sky. As I watched, they swept down over a grove of cottonwoods, rising again with flapping wings as they tried to escape from the attack of a half dozen smaller birds. Over and over again the small birds dove to the attack; occasionally tearing loose feathers that exploded in a fluffy cloud and floated down to earth. Finally, the big hawks had been driven far away from the nests of the feisty defenders, allowing the little birds to return to the cottonwoods.

Reining in the dun, I'd halted and watched this wildlife drama unfold. Time after time, the tiny birds had dived and swooped at their huge enemies, their coordination faultless as they veered off at just the right moment; relentless, as they pestered the larger birds, forcing them to serach elsewhere for easier prey.

I knew that what I had seen took place constantly, in all forms of life, somewhere in the world. A hen pheasant showing a predator what appeared to be a broken wing, to draw it away from her young ones. A weathered farm woman hiding her children, and offering herself to attacking Indians. It was not an exact parallel to my earlier thoughts, but it made me reconsider.

Frank Specter could be the victim and not necessarily the aggressor in these gunfights described by *Harper's*. Younger men, excited by the prospect of being "top gun," would do as those tiny birds had done, but for a different reason. They would seek out men with established reputations, such as the man Frank Specter, and pester and taunt them into a confrontation. If they could win, they would naturally inherit the reputation of the man they had killed. Their egos, inflated by earlier successes with drunks or men of lesser skill, did not permit them even to consider losing....

CHAPTER SIX

For the next three hours, the dun and I covered some real ground. Twice, we came upon small bunches of cattle, mostly cows with young calves. They all looked healthy enough, and were well away from the hedge fences, so I didn't bother the overprotective mother cows.

I found that Judah's ranchland was well watered. Springs and shallow creeks were in abundance, and never did I find a cow very far from water. One of the streams was particularly welcome, since it was well shaded by cottonwoods, and I'd spotted it at a time when both the dun and I were in need of some liquid refreshment. Me! I was parched!

Swinging down from the saddle, I let the horse drink only what I felt he could handle; then slipped the bit and put a picket pin down in the middle of a grassy clearing.

Kneeling down by the creek's edge, I took off my hat and plunged my head under the surface. For over a minute, I held my breath and reveled in the cool, refreshing water. Then, as I straightened, my head streaming, a stiffening of the short hairs on the back of my neck warned me I wasn't alone.

With my bandana, I patted at my face, glancing off to the sides as I did so. I had company, all right! Three of 'em stood close by. Two near the creek, and the third behind the dun, my saddle carbine in his hands. They were Indians, but of what tribe I had no idea.

Carefully, I stood up, and forced a smile. Holding up my right hand in what I felt was a gesture of peace, I began to speak....

"Welcome to my camp. I have no food, but I have tobacco. You are welcome to share." Here, I made a motion towards my shirt pocket, where my pouch and papers were kept.

Apparently, I had interrupted them at the watering place. As we stood there in silence, a fourth Indian came out of an opening in the trees, leading four ponies. I berated myself silently for not noticing pony tracks by the stream. There were plenty, and I could see them plainly now.

The tallest of the four spoke sharply to the one standing by my dun, and he moved several paces to his left. This put him in a position to fire at me without the danger of striking one of his own. As he moved, he opened the carbine's action enough to make certain there was a round in the chamber. Grinning, he looked right at me, and there was no doubt that his intention was to kill me, given the slightest excuse.

The clothing he wore was ragged. Mostly castoffs he had undoubtedly taken from white men, and he didn't look like he had been eating regularly. Slung over his back was a bow of some yellowish wood, and a furred quiver of arrows. A knife was at his belt, but no other gun that I could see.

Mr. Tall Injun wore butternut jeans, and a beaded

vest of deerskin, with long, tubular seashells forming a sort of armored chest covering. His braids were
longer than those of the others, and were wrapped
in red cloth. Thrust down into his waistband was a
cap and ball Colt Army, and suspended from a rawhide thong around his neck was a copper powder
flask.

The Indian holding the ponies was armed with a
lance, but the fourth had a bow, and he was holding
it in readiness, an arrow at the nock. I considered
my chances.... If push came to shove, I figured it
could go my way, providing I took out the one who
had my carbine in the first exchange of shots.

I was sweating now! I really had no idea of how
fast I'd be able to haul my six-gun from the holster,
or if I could be reasonably accurate, once it was free.
But, I wasn't at all frightened! I felt like a finely
tuned instrument, drawn to the stretching point; or
a racehorse, quivering at the gate. It was anticipation
that I was feeling now! Suddenly, like a relaxing
bath, all tension left. The points of my shoulders
dropped. My right hand was poised over the holster,
the arm slightly bent. My breathing was deep and
regular.

The tall one was studying me, and I could tell
my calm assurance had him worried. There were
four armed men against me, and the odds should
have been in their favor. He spoke, and his voice
was deep and resonant. His fingers played idly with
the butt of the revolver in his waistband.

"I am called *Gui-t'ainte*, White Wolf, by my people. I am a Chief of the Kiowa-Apache. These others
ride with me. Is this your range? This land that feeds
the pale buffalo? We look for food for our women
and young ones, but all the game has gone now. In
my boyhood times, this land had many deer and
buffalo. More, even, than the cows that now feed

on the grass. The buffalo were thicker than the hairs on our heads in those times, and we were able to kill many for our food."

As he spoke, my glance had strayed to the ponies. They'd apparently already watered, and now they fidgeted and pawed at the ground, anxious to get to the grass my dun was enjoying. They were all saddled up with the wood and rawhide rigs made and used by the Plains Indian. One of them, a dish-faced roan, was wearing a highly decorated saddle, with intricately fashioned beadwork. One of the stirrups had a long strip of deerskin hanging from it, with a beaded design that showed a manlike figure with blue pants and a red shirt.

"That your horse?" I asked him.

As he stared over toward the roan, a puzzled look on his face, I unbuttoned a shirt pocket, using my left hand. Then I showed him the bit of deerskin I'd picked up some days ago. It seemed to match, perfectly, from where I was standing.

"Found this hanging from a bush, close to two young heifers we'd been led to by birds. Those cows'd been butchered! Whoever did this thing took only the choice cuts of meat.

"To kill the animals of another man for food, when one is starving, that is understood. To take only the tenderest of the meat, leaving the rest for the coyotes, that is stealing! It is also an insult to the owner of those animals."

With an explosive exhalation of breath, the Injun holding my carbine hollered something, and whipped the weapon into a firing position. I heard the hammer clicking to full cock.

As in a dream, I watched my hand come up, and thrust forward, the .44 Colt in my fist. My thumb slipped off the fully cocked hammer, and the gun bucked in recoil, a thunderous roar assaulting my eardrums.

A cloud of dirty white smoke blossomed at the Colt's muzzle, but before it obscured the target, my left hand chopped down, the base of my thumb rolling the hammer back and continuing through as I felt the recoil of my second shot. In the same continuous motion, the heel of my left palm struck the hammer a third time, as I pivoted, firing that round toward the Indian with the strung bow and dropping him where he stood. The first man had been smashed to the ground and lay there, unmoving, the carbine a few feet from his hand.

All this took place in seconds, and left me half deafened, staring over the barrel of my cocked Colt at the tall Indian Chief. An unbelieving look on his face, he was holding that Colt Army, the barrel still pointed at the ground. His mind was telling him to raise the gun and fire, but those muscles refused to respond. As I watched, he lowered the hammer and dropped the gun to the ground.

He wasn't afraid to die. I could see that plainly enough in his resolute stance. But he wasn't a damn fool, either. I motioned to the one with the ponies to drop the lance, and was surprised to see the Indian drop down, arms over head in a position of supplication, and begin to cry. The surprises were complete when Tall Injun ran over and began to comfort the prone figure. It was a woman! The outline of her fully developed breasts was apparent as he raised her to a seated position and pillowed her head on his shoulder. I realized now why he'd dropped the Colt without an argument.

I stood there, punching out the empty hulls and slipping in fresh cartridges. Turning the cylinder to an empty chamber, I lowered the hammer, and holstered the gun. Reaction, the aftermath of all violence, was beginning to set in. The whole thing had taken less than a minute, and two were dead. My icy calm had disappeared. I wasn't shaking, but I should have been. I knew now! I *was* Frank Specter!

CHAPTER SEVEN

WITH A WARNING to the pair on the ground to stay there, I walked over and picked my carbine off the grass. The hammer was down, and a fired round was in the chamber. Apparently he'd gotten off a shot, though I had no recollection of hearing the Winchester fire.

My mind was racing! I had no alternative but to believe that I was the infamous Frank Specter. As yet, nothing came clear. I really knew no more about myself than I had known before the shootings. My past was still a blank, but things were stirring about.

Bending over the first dead man, I pulled aside his shirt, and found what I'd feared was true. There were two holes in his left chest, and they touched each other.... That kind of shooting was not representative of an average man. It would take months or even years of practice to attain the blinding speed, coupled with this degree of killing accuracy.

Point was... now that I knew who I must be, what happened next? What should I do about it? There was still no one to tell me where I even lived!

Whether or not I had a wife and family somewhere, waiting for me to write, or to come home.

One thing sure! If I was Frank Specter, I hadn't drowned in the Mississippi a year ago. What could be the reason for not wanting others to know that I still lived? Had I decided to drop out of sight because I was tired of being a target for every would-be gunslinger who wanted to build a reputation?

Harper's had said Specter was a detective. That he was in the employ of the Pinkerton Agency. Perhaps the story of my drowning was to throw someone off. Make someone feel secure.

My head hurt! The booming explosions of the Colt, added to the muddle of my poor, mixed-up mind, had brought on some aching pains in my skull. Suddenly I realized the man who called himself *Gui-t'ainte* had been speaking for some time, and I hadn't caught what he was saying.

I walked over close to him and the woman, who was no longer crying. He patted her on the shoulder, and they both got to their feet. He appeared calm enough, but showed some concern for his companion. I felt no anger toward them, only pity.

"I'm sorry," I told him. "We are really not enemies, you and I, but you had killed the cattle of my employer. Still, I would not have harmed any of you, if your man had not been so foolish as to try and kill me. He was very young, and I had to kill him to save my own life. The other man was also ready to use his bow, and so he is dead now."

"What will you do with us?" he asked. "To take us to the town is death for us both. The men there will hang us, without even a trial." He turned toward the woman, and put his hand on her shoulder. The tears had left tracks in the dirt on her face, but she was not unattractive. I judged her age at no more than twenty.

"This is my wife, *Pai-t'ene*. In your words, Sun Bird. I must tell you a story now. It is important that you listen to me. You can trust us not to harm you, and you do have my gun."

I had picked up the old revolver, and stuck it in my belt. For the time being, I felt that was the best place for it to be. I glanced up at the sky. Still early in the afternoon, and I wasn't on any schedule.

"I will listen," I told him. "Say what you have to say." I sat down on a large rock in the shade of the trees, reaching into my pocket for the makin's. "Let's hear your story," I said, as I scratched a match for my cigarette. He'd shaken his head when I offered him the tobacco.

"My wife and I have left the Agency. Our people have had their land near the North Fork of the Red River for over six years, and we were keeping the Treaty.

"For some months now, a white man has desired my wife. I could understand this, because she is young and comely, with hair like the wing of a crow. Some of our people do not see wrong in the white man taking our women to use, but my heart cannot allow any man this privilege." He was looking directly into my eyes as he spoke, and now his face wrinkled into laugh lines, as he continued.

"You and I are of an age. Have you ever had the pleasure of watching a young girl grow into womanhood? To see her as a child, curious and inquisitive, as she learns of life? My Sun Bird was only seven when I first became aware of her.

"Her father *Gi-edal* and another were killed nine years ago, as we were bringing stolen horses back from a raid into New Mexico. Some others were wounded by the soldiers, and I was one of those. The mother of Sun Bird cared for me when the soldiers returned us to Fort Sill, and healed my wounds.

When I could stand without assistance, I took her to wife."

He lifted his shoulders and gestured toward the pocket where I kept the tobacco. "Perhaps I will share smoke," he told me. "We have been without for some time now."

The woman took a beaded bag from inside her clothing and got out a stubby pipe, carved from what appeared to be a red root of some kind. He accepted it from her and packed some of my tobacco into the bowl, using a thumb and forefinger.

I scratched a match on my bootsole and held it, while he got the pipe going. He peered up at me, his eyes slitted under heavy brows. For a moment, our gaze locked in mutual appraisal, then he stepped back a pace and sank to the ground, sitting with his legs crossed. Sun Bird sat behind him, the garment she was wearing pulled partially over her head.

His eyes closed as he savored the first puff, and he nodded in appreciation. Another, drawn slowly through the stem and exhaled through his nose; then he continued....

"The mother had more years then I, but she had grace, and the understanding of woman and man things. Though I was already a warrior, having taken coups, I was not familiar with women. She could not survive, without a hunter to bring the food and to protect her and her child. So, she came to me, in the darkness of her lodge, and we were as one.

"We were very happy, and when the White Soldier Chief decided to give us the land on Red River, we went there with a feeling that peace was complete."

He stopped talking for a moment, and drew in a puff, letting it trickle out through his nostrils. "Ahh!" he murmured. "That is good!"

"So..." he continued. "Sun Bird grew to womanhood, as my foster daughter. She was a happy child. The creatures were all her friends, but most of all, she loved the birds. With them, she could spend many hours; watching them glide across the sky, and perhaps wishing she could join them in flight.

"Two years ago, when Sun Bird had seen fifteen summers, a bad fever came among our people. My wife, the mother of Sun Bird, became very sick, and was one of the first to die. In a dream, she saw *Gadombit-souhi*, Old Woman Under the Ground, a strong medicine of our people. Standing on a flat rock, a white wolfskin over her shoulders, the old woman was no bigger than a small dog, and her hair flowed to the ground. In a loud voice, she told my wife that she must die, and that I would take Sun Bird in her place. This was a good thing, because she could go to the Spirit World knowing that Sun Bird would be cared for and loved.

"All went well for us, though no children came to gladden our marriage. I was made a Chief of the *Nadi-isha-Dena*, the Principal People, as we Kiowa-Apaches call ourselves. Working with the tribal police, I helped to keep the Texas herds from intruding on our grass. I also attended the school for a time, where I learned to speak better the language of the white man.

"Then came a trader. Goldman, he called himself. He was a small man, but worked very hard. He built a store there, and stocked it with many things our women wanted. Cloth and beads, and many pretty things made of silver. Kettles that were made of black iron, knives that were sharp, and needles of all sizes.

"Many of our women would give themselves to this man, and their Indian husbands would turn their heads, so long as the trade goods were given in exchange. I saw this thing happen to them, but kept my own counsel.

"When this trader spoke to my wife, she ran from him, and would no longer go to his store. Then he came to me, and a fine Winchester rifle was in his hand. There were deer, and many flowers carved in the metal, and it gleamed with silver and gold. He told me that he wanted Sun Bird to be his wife, and that he would give me the rifle and many shells for her. He was tired of having different women, and wanted one to be his alone.

"I asked Sun Bird to tell me if this was what she wanted to do, and she looked at me with tears, and said she was the wife of a chief. That she would kill herself before allowing this white man, or any man, to touch her in the marriage way.

"Politely, I explained this to the trader, Goldman. When he became very angry and used many bad words, I told him to leave my lodge and never enter again. This he did, but the desire for my wife still burned in him.

"In late Spring, we made ready to meet the Texas drovers as they brought their cattle through our lands. My wife had fears for her safety while I was away, but I assured her we had nothing to worry about. The old men and boys would protect her, and the other women, and I'd never be over a day's ride away from our home.

"On the fourth morning, my pony stepped in a hole, spraining a leg badly. It was a fine animal, and the best of all my horseherd, so I decided to return to the camp. What is a day's ride becomes two days, if you must walk. I came back to my home in the darkness of night, and Man Above was guiding my footsteps, because I walked softly.

"I saw the strange horse tethered behind our lodge, and I heard sounds like an animal breathing after a long chase in the forest. Forgetting my arms, I ran inside.

"The trader, Goldman, had entered our tipi, and had taken Sun Bird's clothing from her body. He had struck her with a club, and she was like a dead person. In my grief and rage, I struck him to the ground; then lifted him high in the air, and broke him over my knee like a dry piece of wood.

"Sun Bird was not dead, and when she awakened, we considered this thing I had done. The Soldier Chief would perhaps believe me, when I told him how Goldman had tried to harm my wife. But he could not allow me to go unpunished for killing a white man. So we packed some few things, and left the Agency, and our people, forever.

"We came upon these two you have killed, while camping in the hills. They are not Kiowa-Apaches. They come from some mountains toward the west, and call themselves *Nun'z*. Your name for them is Ute. That one you shot first was crazy. I could not control him, and soon would have killed him myself had you not done so. The other was his younger brother, and he would follow anywhere, so long as he had a leader.

"Now! You have heard my story. Answer my question! Say what you will do with us!"

I wasn't feeling nearly as sorry for myself as I had before. Far as I could see, there was no solution to the situation that this man and his wife were facing. Sure, they could keep on running and hiding out like animals, but that could not go on forever. They were Indians, and as such had no chance of avoiding capture....

That was the answer! A plan was forming in my thoughts. Somewhere I remembered reading; "If you can't beat 'em, join 'em." It would take some doing, and I'd have to convince my friend, Judah, but it *could* be done. Or could it? Persuading Judah to help Indians, considering his hatred and grief, after what had happened to his wife...Would he even listen to such a plan? I decided I'd better think on it, but in the meantime, they had to have a place to stay and food to eat.

"Look," I told him. "I believe your story, and don't you worry about me taking you to Dodge City. Matter of fact, it probably would be tough going, because I doubt you'd come along willingly, and I'd wind up having to kill you both. Am I not right?"

The look on their faces confirmed what I'd just said. In spite of the fact that they were unarmed, and had watched me demonstrate my skill with a gun, no way could I have persuaded them to face angry white cowmen.

"I have a plan, and it will work, but first I must ask my employer for his help. He has suffered greatly, from something done many years ago. He lost his wife when a band of renegade Indians raided this ranch. They were led by a murderous white man, but my friend seeks his revenge by killing Indians. I believe he can be made to change his ways."

"We believe you," said White Wolf. "After all, what else can we do? You could kill us where we stand, and no others would blame you. What is your plan? Tell us what we can do now to save our lives."

"Look," I told him. "You speak the language of the white man very well. Better than most whites on this frontier. I feel that you could pass for white with very little trouble. You'd have to cut your hair short, part it on the side; then with a hat covering most of it, no one would know the difference. Proper clothing won't be hard to come by, and you are already wearing white men's pants.

"Main thing now is to find a place where you can stay in hiding, until I can make all the arrangements.

It could take a week, maybe longer. This place is no good. Too many cows water here, and the men who work for my friend wouldn't feel as I do. They would see you only as an enemy, or a trespasser, and treat you accordingly."

Sun Bird nudged her husband, and spoke a few words in his ear. He nodded, and a smile flitted across his face. Turning to me, he explained.

"There is a cave in the hills, and it is not too far from this place. We stayed there a few days ago, but became very nervous because it was so close to this ranch. Also, there were signs that many fires had been built in that cave; some very recent. We will take the chance. The cave is big enough to conceal our horses during the day, and we can take them out at night to feed." He paused...looked over at me for a moment, then continued....

"Those cows that you found...You were very angry at the wasted meat. Let me explain why there was no more taken.

"When we killed the two young cows, I used my revolver on one of them. The sound of the shot must have carried a long distance, and it was heard by a white man. Before we'd even started to dress them out, we saw him coming. It was an old man in a wagon. He was very thin, and had white hair. That first man you killed wanted to shoot him and take the team, but I said no. He would be missed, and then the white soldiers would hunt us down, wherever we would go.

"Quickly, we took meat that was easy to cut out, and rode away, keeping to the trees for some miles until we were far from that place. The old man never saw us."

I nodded. Sounded like Rufus Shelby, the old man I'd met on the road to Dodge. Judah had said Shelby's property bordered on his own. Knowing that the old man could be nearby made me wonder at the risk we were taking. But I knew of no other way to save White Wolf and Sun Bird. I pulled his Colt out of my belt, and handed it over.

"Here!" I told him. "You'll need this gun. Now, how far away is this cave you were talking about? Whereabouts does it lie from here?"

He thrust the revolver down behind his belt and pointed. "To the west, where the sun sets. It is maybe one hour ride from this place. There are patches of trees, like this one, and we can keep from sight most of the way."

"Okay," I said. "Now here's what we're going to do. You will need meat for perhaps a week, so I will find a steer to butcher. You and your wife will go ahead, and I will follow with the animal. We won't kill the steer until we are safe in the cave. Do you understand?"

He made a sign yes, and pointed at the two bodies. "What must we do about these? Soon the birds will come, and they would be a signal to the white men."

"Bury them back under the trees, and pile some stones so the coyotes won't dig them out. That one has a knife, which you will need. Keep the bows and anything else you feel will come in handy for the next week or so. After you get them buried, wait in the trees until I return."

I pulled my picket pin, got the bit into the dun's mouth, and tightened the cinches. Stepping up into the saddle and taking up the reins, I looked down at the Indian couple.

"Everything's going to work out just fine. Don't you two worry about a thing. Trust me!"

I nudged the dun into a lope, and we headed out. About a mile or so farther on, I found a bunch of Judah's beef, feeding in a hollow. There wasn't any

steers among them, but I spotted a runty bull grazing
on the rim. Looked to be less than two years old,
and not one Judah would use for breeding stock.
Probably a "dogie" that had been missed at roundup.
An orphan calf that had hidden from the riders.

The dun and I rode around the hollow and flanked
him. I put the horse up the bank, and he got on that
bull's tail in a flash, his teeth only inches away. "If
you want a horse to cut cattle, find one that hates
cows...." Now what ever made me think that? The
thought had just popped into my mind, as we got
after the bull.... Something from my unknown past.

The little animal was using every trick to evade
my horse, but every time he dodged, the dun anticipated the move, keeping close behind him. The
other cattle looked up, then kept right on grazing.
After a pass or two, we got him lined out in the
direction we wanted to go, and I just sat back while
my horse did all the work. Once, I stood up in the
stirrups and looked all around. No other riders were
in sight, so it seemed safe enough to go on with the
plan.

As I neared the tree-lined creek, I saw the Indian
couple riding out with the two extra ponies led behind. One waved at me, then turned and went on.

From the sun's position, I figured it was close on
to two o'clock, and I had plenty of time yet. Nancy
never fed supper much before six, giving the hands
plenty of time to wash up before eating. I wondered
how I would feel at the table, knowing now my true
identity. Would I be able to keep quiet about my
discoveries? Would I lie, if it came to that, without
giving myself away? I shook off my feelings of dis-
quiet, and concentrated on the job at hand. That of
getting to the cave safely with this beef, and being
able to help my new-found friends.

I considered that for a moment. Under a different

set of circumstances, would I still be as anxious to help these two Indians? If it were not for the fact that I was lost myself, lost in a blurred maze of no memory, with no one to guide me toward the road back. Would I then be as willing to help?

We were coming up on a line of hills now, and ahead of me the two riders had angled off to the right. A moment later, they disappeared from view. I went on, the dun making sure the bull kept going in a straight line.

As the horse lunged at the steeper ground with his hindquarters bunched, I saw White Wolf looking down from the crest of the hill. There was a big smile on his face, and he held up one arm in greeting. With his help, we cornered the bull on a narrow bench, where I was able to get my rope on his forefeet and throw him down. The Indian sprang off his pony in a flash, and sat on the bull's head long enough to draw a knife across his throat.

He loosened my loop, and we let the animal kick as I coiled my rope. In a few moments, he lay quiet, and we watched as Sun Bird began to butcher the beef. In a very short time, she had the hide off, and laid to one side, where she piled the portions of cut meat. White Wolf and I lugged the heavy hindquarters back into the cave, only a few feet away. I was impressed. It was a big cave! The hobbled ponies were back in the rear, and seemed content enough. A pile of grass lay on the ground in front of them, and they were chomping away like they'd lived in caves all of their lives.

Back outside, Sun Bird was finished with the bull. She'd laid out the loins, heart, liver and entrails on the hide, a cloud of flies hovering over the bloody pile. As I watched, White Wolf turned the liver over, and separated a green sack from the underside with his knife.

Next, he cut off a generous portion of the raw liver, and squeezed a few drops on it from the pear-shaped sack. With one hand rubbing his flat stomach, he made a smacking noise with his lips, and grinned broadly.

"Very good to eat," he told me. "Here! You try! You'll be surprised at how good this will taste." He held the raw, bloody chunk of fresh liver out toward me.

"Nah.... Thanks, anyway," I told him. "I'll be having my supper, soon's I get back to the ranch house. You go ahead. You and Sun Bird need all the nourishment you can get."

"There is plenty," he countered. "We can't eat all of it before it spoils. It's rich, and very good for the blood." He held it out again, and reluctantly I put it in my mouth.

I chewed for a moment. It *was* surprisingly tasty! Those few drops of gall had seasoned it, delicately, and found the full flavor of the liver. I licked my fingers, but held one hand up in refusal as he offered me another piece. My neckerchief served as a napkin.

The tall Indian and I carried the balance of the meat into the cave, using the hide as a big sack. Sun Bird had already gotten a fire going just inside the entrance, where a lot of smoke couldn't be seen. As I stood there, she started cutting up meat in preparation for their meal.

"Best be on my way," I told them. "You folks stick close to this cave, and I'll get back to you, soon's I can."

The dun and I half slid down the hillside, and I waved at them when we reached the bottom. My horse must have had an idea we were headed for home, because he stepped right on out at a run, and fought it when I reined him back. Finally, we agreed on a fast singlefoot that covered lots of ground in a hurry. Looking up at the sky, I figured it was about an hour until supper time. Sort of wished I'd taken another chunk of that tasty liver. I hadn't eaten anything since breakfast.

CHAPTER EIGHT

AFTER SUPPER, I asked Judah what he had in mind for me to do the next day. I'd already explained my absence by telling him I'd wanted to familiarize myself with the ranch. At this point, I wasn't ready to mention my Injun friends. His reply was a welcome one because it could give me the opportunity to pick up the clothing I needed for them.

"Me and Bud are ridin' over to Hodgeman's place tomorrow, to see what he's got to sell in the brood bulls we're thinkin' about usin' to start our young heifers. We'll take just two of the boys with us, and figger on gittin' back Tuesday, sometime before supper.

"Buck's gonna strawboss the rest of the crew; roundin' up another one hundred two-year-old heifers, and takin' them to the four sections we got under fence, up in the high pasture. I plan to buy fifteen of them small Angus bulls, if old man Hodgeman's willin' to part with that many. Bud has figgered on four, but with two hundred head already there, it'll take at least fifteen bulls, so's to be sure of at least a seventy percent calf crop.

"Charley Fong's got him a grocery list 'bout a mile long, and I'd be obliged if you'd give Nancy a hand with it. Take more'n the buckboard to haul all that stuff, so you'd better take the big spring wagon and use them mules I keep in the barn. They'll outpull any horse team on the place. My girl can handle the shoppin', so's all you gotta do is load it up and drive the team."

He looked across the table at me. "How's that head feelin' now? Still givin' you some hurt?"

I told him it was just fine, and the hair was even beginning to cover the scars.

"Nancy did a fine job, Judah. Doc McCarty couldn't leave a more satisfied patient, and I'm sure his prices are higher than her's."

"Well, then. The boys've brought in a nice chestnut, and put him in the corral. It's a gelding, and he shows lots of saddle marks, so he's been ridden. Not a brand on him, anywhere, so we can't tell where he's come from. Looks like it could be a good cowhorse, and I can't stand seein' one go to waste." He paused; and looked down the table. Buck was gazing off into the distance, and the others seemed to be studying something on their plates, because none of them bothered to look up. Judah cleared his throat, then went on talking.

"Seem's the rest of the boys'll be busy, so why don't you put a saddle on him and take out whatever kinks he's hidin' under that peaceable exterior. Horse like him'd really come in mighty handy at roundup, this fall. If you're still workin' here then, you can add him to your string. Start on him when you git back from Dodge, and you can finish off Tuesday. Plenty of time to gentle him down enough to use on cows."

"Sure, Judah," I replied. "Be glad to give him a try. I been kinda wondering if maybe I hadn't worked myself out of a job, now that we've finished the squeezer. Don't want you keeping me on here just because I'm broke."

"Oh! Don't you worry none. You'll be earning your money. You can count on that, Case. This ain't no grub-line outfit. There's plenty to do, for a man who's willin' to work." The gaze went around the table, again....

"And that's more'n I can say for some others," he finished off.

I nodded.... As I looked around the table, I could see my friends all had strange expressions. Some of 'em, Buck included, seemed to be holding their breath. At least one was turning purple. I decided maybe I'd best take a look at the chestnut, 'cause I sure didn't seen anything funny in what my friend Judah had just said....

Nancy was starting to clear off the table, so I piled the plates closest to me on my own and stacked the cups. Shoving back my chair, I stood up and carried the stack out into the kitchen. Nancy was right behind with the remainder.

It was very warm, and beads of perspiration were apparent on her pretty face. She wiped her eyes with the apron.

"Whew! If it gets any hotter in here, I'm going to wilt. Charley! Why don't you do your cooking outside, like you do on roundup? Must be over a hundred or more!"

She thanked me for helping her with the dishes. "Maybe I *will* hire another Chinaman," she told me with a wry smile.

"What time do you want to head in to Dodge?" I asked. "We might get an early start, if you don't mind. Your dad's got another chore for me when we get back, and I'd like as much time as possible to get it done. I've a hunch it's not so easy as it sounds."

She looked at me questioningly.... "Why? What is it he wants you to do?"

I explained about the chestnut. "It sounds sorta routine, but Buck and the rest seemed to be sharing some private joke. They were having a hard time not laughing out loud, there at the table. Also, I noticed that Buck, and one of the others, looked like they'd been in a knock-down, drag-out, when they washed up before supper. Could be they've already tried a ride on that horse, and didn't do so well."

"Maybe you better check with dad, before you ride a risky horse. I'm sure he isn't a party to the joke, if that's all they have in mind for you."

"No! Let's just leave it stand as it is. Be lots worse my running to the boss. I'll make out just fine," I assured her. "Who knows, maybe I was a bronc rider in my past."

Taking off her apron, Nancy got down two clean cups. "I'm going to have another cup of coffee and take a walk. Would you like to come along?" she asked.

Buck had already asked me if I'd liked to join in on the bunkhouse poker game that evening. "Payday's two weeks off, so we'll have to play 'jawbone,' and pay later. Who knows," he'd said. "Mebbe you were a cardslick, 'stead of a drummer peddlin' guns." I'd said I'd think about it.

Right now, walking with Nancy seemed more fun, so I helped her fill the cups and we went out into the back. Off to the west, the sun was slipping out of sight, and the lengthening shadows cast long, probing fingers across the bareness of the ranchyard. Horses, wagons, and the constant tread of the men had packed the earth hard as adobe, and not a blade of grass could poke through. In contrast was the carefully tended plot in front, with its bright greenery and the profusion of flowers I'd seen on that first day.

I stole a look at Nancy out of the corner of my eye. Even with her hair in disarray and her frock wrinkled from working in the ranch kitchen, she was beautiful. Taller than the average woman, she walked with a sureness of purpose, reaching out with a lithe stride almost as long as mine. On the edge of the clearing where her mother was buried, she stopped and leaned back against a tree. Her full figure was in perfect outline beneath the thin cotton dress, but she appeared unaware of this as she sipped her coffee.

"Have you seen what lies beyond these trees?" Her query, spoken over the rim of her cup, was low-voiced. "My murdered mother, killed when I was only a child, is buried there."

"I know," I told her. "I came back here the first morning, and saw the grave. Your dad told me the story, when we were on our way into Dodge. He's gotten his revenge, with a great deal of interest, over the past eighteen years."

She nodded. "Yes. But not without paying the price. It weighed heaviest on him after the last Indian was killed. He was very young, or so my father told me one night. A young man who was trying to prove to his tribe that he was a warrior. He fought bravely, but didn't have a chance in a battle with the man-wolf, as they have named my father...."

She sighed.... "I really believe that he is sorry now. I feel he would rather forget, and never kill another Indian."

"How do you feel about them?" I asked, and was surprised at her answer.

"I wished there was something I could do to help," she replied. "I can't honestly blame a whole people for what one small group did to my mother. Besides, they were led by one of our own race; a so-called white man! We call him a renegade, and not representative of all whites. Surely we find good and bad in both races." She looked up at me in appeal.

I nodded in agreement. "Yes," I told her. "We must also remember that we are the intruders, and in their country. I also agree that everyone must be treated as an individual."

The twilight had faded fast, the shadows deepening. . . . We were close; and in the nearness of her fragrance, a scent of lilac soap, fresh-baked bread, and mint-sweet breath, I leaned forward, the impulse to take her in my arms, and to kiss her soft lips, almost overwhelming me.

Then reality took over. Fat chance I had of ever winning a prize like Nancy Clayton! Me? A killer! A man who had a record of ten dead men hanging around his neck? Whose occupation was seeking out men to kill them. Who couldn't even remember where he lived, or where he was born. A man with no prospects for the future, except perhaps words without regret, chiseled on a granite marker.

This was a nice girl. She wouldn't even be standing here with me if she knew who I really was, and had been. Didn't make any difference, no matter what the circumstance before, I had no business even considering a relationship with her.

Nancy had apparently been lost in thought, like me. Perhaps she sensed some of what I had considered. At any rate, she pointed over toward a fallen tree trunk. . . .

"Would you like to stay out here for a few more minutes?" she asked. "It's such a nice evening that I hate for it to be wasted. We've had precious few chances to talk with each other, and I know so little about you. Sorry, Case. That was the wrong thing to say. I am sorry, honest. It's too darn bad, not being able to even tell a girl your real name. Well, it can't last forever, we know that. You'll be your old self again, and this'll all be just a bad memory."

"Sure, Nancy. Some day. Tell me more about how you think the Indians should be treated. Did you ever know one? Ever had a chance to talk with an Injun, up real close?"

She nodded. We'd seated ourselves on the fallen tree, me being careful not to sit too close. I wondered if I'd known many women, as Frank Specter. Right now, I felt like it was my first time out. I listened, as she began again....

"When I went to school in Kansas City, I shared a room in the dormitory with three other girls. One was a pure-blooded Osage Indian. Her father was a chief of that tribe. We had both grown up on the plains, and shared many similar experiences with animals and people. In a very short time, we became the best of friends. We actually were closer than two sisters. I never did think of her as a savage. As a matter of fact, my skin was much darker than hers, since I'd been such a tomboy on the ranch.

"We cried when school came to an end for the year, and I could hardly wait for the next term. On graduation day, her parents came for the ceremony, as did my father. I tried so hard to persuade him to meet them, but he wouldn't even consider such a thing." She paused, remembering.

"She's married now, and I don't hear from her very often. Her husband is a white man, and they own a ranch in Montana. Apparently that's fairly common up there, and they haven't had to face any criticism from their neighbors."

She turned to face me. "Here I am...rambling

on and on, when I can tell that you have a reason for asking me why I'd welcome a chance to help the Indians. C'mon, Case. Tell me all about it."

Her demand took me unawares. I should have realized that she would sense an underlying reason for my swinging the conversation to Indians. How much dare I tell her? Certainly not the location of the cave where my new friends were hiding. But what harm would there be in just relating part of the story, minimizing my part in the shoot-out. Perhaps, if I'd leave out the two dead Indians altogether... That had to be the answer! Then there'd be no mention of my prowess with a six-gun, and how I'd come to be that fast and accurate.

"You win, Nancy. You're right, I do have a reason, and a good one. It involves some very real Indians, and a problem we might be able to overcome for them, if you're willing.

"Now I'm not going to ask for promises of silence, and my story isn't going to be a complete one. What I do tell you can't harm those involved, only me. If you decide to run to your father with this, I might get sent on my way, but these Indians won't be any worse off than they are now. Will you be satisfied with that? Later, I'll give you the whole tale, if you are still interested. Okay?"

She agreed, and I proceeded to tell her about White Wolf and his pretty wife, Sun Bird. How the trader had attempted to victimize them, and the killing that had been forced on a man who wanted peace.

Nancy listened in silence, until I came to the part when White Wolf had found his wife unconscious and on the point of being ravished.

"That's awful," she cried. "That man was no better than those beasts who raided this ranch, and killed my mother! I want to help them all I can. I must help them!"

"Well, you can begin tomorrow, by helping me to get those articles of clothing they'll need. I've still got most all my pay from last month, but it may not be enough. Then too, I might have run into trouble trying to buy a dress. You'll have to handle that."

"Don't you worry about a thing, Case. Mercy! I can hardly wait! That poor girl! Let's leave early tomorrow. You give me a hand with my chores, and we'll get started, soon's breakfast's over, and the dishes cleared away."

She reached up and took me by the arms, gripping me with tensed fingers.

"Case," she said. "You're a fine man! I'm proud to be a friend of yours. You won't regret taking me into your confidence. You just wait and see!"

Up on her tiptoes, she kissed me on my cheek, then turned and ran back to the house. I stood there for a moment, rubbing the spot where her lips had touched. Then once more, I felt the blackness of frustration and despair. The truth of my identity as Frank Specter descended like a cloud.

CHAPTER NINE

I ROLLED OUT early Monday morning. As yet, Judah hadn't said anything about me moving to the bunk-house, so the spare bedroom in the house was still mine. Since Nancy and I were going in to Dodge, I decided to wear my own outfit. That one in which I'd awakened, lying alongside the railroad tracks.

Nancy had sponged off the accumulation of cinder and coal dust, and pressed the pants and vest. It was a lightweight but serviceable wool suit in a brown color, and bore the label of a New York firm. Of course, that didn't necessarily mean that I'd purchased the clothing in New York. It was possible to buy Eastern-tailored suits all over the West. Was it? I guessed so, because that notion popped into my head when I read the label. Another memory from my past...

My borrowed jacket I decided not to take. My vest should more than suffice on these warm June days. A quick glance in the washstand mirror showed me to be neat enough to escort a young lady in to town. Spurs I wouldn't need, since I would be using the spring wagon, but I did buckle on my gunbelt.

Downstairs I stuck my head in through the kitchen

door. Nancy was setting out the tableware, and Charley Fong stood by the massive cook range, turning beefsteaks in a pan.

"I'm gonna go grain the mules, and get the wagon and harness ready," I told her. "What was it you wanted me to help you with this morning?"

"Well, it's something that no self-respecting cowman gets caught doing," she retorted. "Milking a cow! Grab that tin bucket, and see how much you can squeeze outta old Bossy. I got her staked out, in that pasture behind the barn. Here! Take this basket along with you. When you finish milking, I need more eggs for breakfast, so gather what you can, out in the henhouse.

"Wait! Take this dried ear of corn. Bossy won't let her milk down until you give her that." She brushed a wisp of hair out of her eyes as she handed me the corn.

"Say! You look mighty handsome this morning! That suit fits you well, and I like the color. Shame you're going out and waste it on an old milk cow." She laughed, and I couldn't help joining in.

"Serves me right," I told her. "I forgot there's always plenty to do around this place. I'll try and be careful."

I accepted a cup of hot coffee from her and took it with me. On the porch, I stopped for a minute and sipped at the steaming liquid. Down by the bunkhouse I could see some of the crew lined up at the wash basins, Buck among them, and I could hear the shouts of laughter as someone told a joke.

How simple and uncomplicated my life would be if I could just change places with one of them, and not have the threat of Frank Specter's past hanging over my head. Not have some would-be gunslick calling me out. Right now, I was safe. I wasn't known in Ford County. But how long could that last?

It was a unique situation. Here I was, wanting to find a clue to my past, but fearing to have others know who I really must be. Well, I had to stop worrying. Worry would not get any work done.

Bossy and I got along just fine, and I almost filled that bucket. I was a little awkward, but soon got the milk flowing strong. In collecting the eggs, I ran into one brooding hen that objected to me robbing her nest, but I just boosted her out of the way and took all of the eggs.

When I mentioned that to Nancy, she made me take them all back. Seems they were a little old to fry. She told me the fresher eggs could be found in the grass around the henhouse, and to bring her some of those.

After breakfast I harnessed up the mules, and we started out toward Dodge. It was another beautiful day, with not a cloud in the sky. Nancy had brought along some coffee left over from breakfast, so we sipped on that as we drove along the dusty road.

Nancy wore a sunbonnet matching the simple blue frock, the same one she had worn that first day. Her arms were bare, showing silky fuzz that glistened in the sun. Peeking out from under the hem were the scuffed tips of her stock boots. My thoughts were wandering, and I couldn't help but daydream; a dream that seemed almost real, with her beside me. Nancy, a small place of our own, and the whole future ahead of us...

"Penny for your thoughts! I hope you are not going to be this quiet all the way to Dodge," she teased.

"Uhh? Oh! Sorry, Nancy. Reckon I had my mind a million miles away. You know, I been thinking. It wouldn't pay for that Injun couple to hang around here, even if they do get a new identity. They really have no money, and he wouldn't be able to fool fellows he was working with for long. Seems a shame they couldn't go on up into Montana, or someplace like that, where being an Indian doesn't make that much of a difference. You know. Like that friend you told me about."

She grinned at me. "Where's your optimism? You went way out on a limb to get them this far, and now you're worrying about a little thing like finding them a place to live. You just trust your foxy old Aunt Nancy, y'hear?"

"Yes, Ma'am!" I chuckled...."You are a wonder, Nancy. I reckon you're about the most optimistic person in the whole state of Kansas. Last night you were cheering me up when I was downhearted about my memory, or lack of one. Now, we've gotten ourselves involved in a conspiracy to help an escaped murderer, who also happens to be a ward of the government, a Federal fugitive to boot. Wait now!" I threw up my arm....

"I'm sorry! I take back that word, 'murderer'. I'd have done the same thing that he did. Maybe worse! Point is, I talked you into helping me, and now I'm having some doubts."

"Look!" Her expression was serious. "We think we are doing the right thing, and we know that what happened back there at the Agency was justified. White Wolf was only doing what any man would do. Protecting one that he loved.

"Now, we have a chance to restore his belief in the peace he cherished. Also to save two valuable lives that have no chance, without our help. We're gonna do it, Case!"

"Right you are!" I snapped the ends of the lines on the near mule's ample bottom. "Hrrrup there, mules! Git to goin' there, mules!" The astonished pair broke into a gallop, but I sawed 'em down to a fast trot. The wagon bounced and swayed across the deeply rutted road.

"Wheee! That's more like it, Case! You gotta talk tough to those mules. That's all they understand!"

I looked over.... Hanging on to the wagon seat with one of her hands, and holding down her bonnet with the other, Nancy was having the time of her life! Her eyes were shining, and her mouth was open in a joyous whoop.

"Hey!" she hollered. "Don't slow down now. This is real great! Almost like flying!"

"Yeah," I told her. "We'll wind up with a couple of wind-broke mules. Dodge'll still be there, when we pull in. The team and wagon belong to your daddy. You too, for that matter. I'd just as soon they were in one piece, when we drive back into the ranch yard."

The rest of that drive was pure pleasure. We chattered away like a couple of kids, all the way into town. I'd have died smiling at any time. She was so much fun to be with. Looking on the bright side of most everything, and a willing listener, though I had little to talk about.

Her own life had been a happy one. Raised by a fine man who spared nothing in bringing her whatever she desired, she had remained unspoiled. She wasn't even aware of her beauty, or if she was, didn't dwell on it. Her loveliness reflected the warm glow of happiness within her, and her love of life that showed in her wish to believe, no matter what the circumstance.

Most of the traffic on the road was outbound. Some of my pride must have showed, because most everyone waved, or called out a greeting. A few riders looked like they might have spent the night in jail, or passed out in an alley, but they all tried to smile through the pain. One good thing about a lost memory, I couldn't remember ever having a hangover....

"First stop will be Wright and Beverly's, Case. We buy all our staples from Uncle Bob. It's almost next door to the Long Branch saloon; if you'd like you could drink a beer, while I'm shopping."

"Fine," I replied. "Maybe I'll do just that. Though the last time I tried to walk through their door, some fellow in his cups objected."

"Oh? Well, what happened? Why would anyone object?"

"Nothing much, Nancy." I was sorry now that I'd mentioned my incident with the drunk. "He changed his mind when I chided him about it. No harm done."

She was persistent, and tried her best to pry more out of me, but we drew up in front of the store about then. Quick-like, I set the brake and jumped down. Offering my hand, I helped her to the ground.

The mercantile was an imposing structure for a Western cowtown. The walls were of brick, and it stood two stories. On one side was a flight of outside stairs, which I assumed led up to an apartment or some sort of living quarters.

"Look, Case!" Nancy grabbed me by the arm. "Look at the wagon, over there by the stairs. C'mon, let's take a closer peek!" She dragged me through the throng of pedestrians on the crowded boardwalk, around to the side of the building.

The wagon she had seen was a medium-sized one, with sides built up higher than normal and a canvas cover strung over wooden bows. It was the same one Judah and I had seen, coming into Dodge that day. The painted sign, HEADED HOME, was still in evidence on the sides. Propped on the seat, a card read, FOR SALE —CHEAP—INQUIRE WITHIN.

"That's it, Case! That's it! See! I told you we'd find a way! Let's go find out what they want for it."

Bewildered, I let her drag me into the front entrance. A tall, rawboned man of about forty or so stood near the end of an aisle in earnest conversation with two others. Glancing up at our noisy entrance, he waved to the excited girl I had beside me.

"Hello, Nance! I'll be with you in a minute. Soon's I'm finished here."

Nancy dragged my head down, and whispered hoarsely in my ear. "Let me do all the talking, and don't act surprised, no matter what I say. D'you understand? No matter what…"

I nodded dumbly. I had no idea what she planned, but it would be a surprise, I had no doubt of that. In spite of myself, I had to chuckle. She was something else! Her enthusiasm was boundless! Life with a vibrant girl like her had to be an endless chain of happy surprises.

The conversation in the back had ended, and they were all nodding and shaking hands. The man who had called out was striding toward us, a big smile wreathing his face, and his arms outstretched.

"Nancy girl! What are you doing in Dodge? Seems like at least a year since we saw you last. How have you been?"

"Fine, Uncle Bob. Just fine. I want to introduce you to a friend of mine. Case, here, is one of Dad's new riders."

She pushed me forward and I held out my hand. "Pleasure, Mr. Wright. Quite a place you have here. Looks like you've got a little bit of everything. Must do quite a business."

Wright's grip was strong and dry. His disarming grin was one to inspire confidence in the man, and I right away liked him.

"Heard about you, Case," he told me. "From what I heard, it doesn't pay to push you around. I'd have given a dollar to have seen that ruckus."

Nancy pushed right in.... "What ruckus? What sort of nonsense are you two talking about? C'mon, now. 'Fess up. If you don't I'm going to be very angry!"

"Wasn't nothing, Nancy," I told her. "Forget it, because it's really not important. Isn't that right, sir?" I looked meaningfully at Bob Wright.

He smiled ruefully. "We might's well tell her. She can be very persuasive, whether you know it or not."

He turned to Nancy and very briefly sketched out the incident with the black-bearded drunk. "He'll know better, if there's ever a next time," he told her. "Case, here, didn't waste words with him. Gave him the beating of his life, and in about thirty seconds flat. Imagine! Lying on the walk, half-stunned, after the man had caught him unawares, knocked him down, and started to put the boots to him. My hat's off to you, Case. That's one licking that was well deserved."

Nancy snorted! "Huh! Is that all? Why I thought some of your town laws had been violated. It's the nature of strong men to battle, and I've always figured it was a welcome sort of blow-off valve. Lets them blow off steam. Get problems out in the open, where they can be dealt with." She put her hand on my arm with a prideful expression.

"That man's lucky to have gotten off as easily as he did," she continued. Case is a man! A strong man! He fights for what's right in this world, never losing sight of his ideals. He could take a licking from a better man, and shake his hand, afterwards. That's the measure of a real man!"

I looked at her in some surprise. Here I'd been reluctant to let her find out at all, and she was glorying in the fact that I had beaten a man senseless. A drunk who more'n likely wouldn't even remember what had happened, or care, for that matter. I decided that I couldn't second-guess a woman any better than I could a horse.

"Uncle Bob, we were looking at that wagon you have on the side of the store. The used one, with the motto on the canvas cover. Case is going to need one about that size, soon, and we were wondering how much you planned to ask for it. I know you have to make a profit, but Case is a good friend of the family." She looked up at Wright with such a demure expression that I had to bite my tongue to keep from smiling.

"Well, Nancy, I got that old wagon in trade for groceries. The folks that had it came out here from way down in Biloxi, Mississippi. Seems the feller's brother had started up some sort of farm, down south and east of here, and he needed the extra help to keep it going, so he sent them money they needed for the trip. He's got two wagons, but was running a little short of grub. We traded.

"It's an old one, made by the Studebaker Brothers in eighteen seventy-two. One of the first made, at their branch plant in St. Joe. We looked it over pretty good, and the running gear is in crackerjack shape. Needs a board replaced, here and there, but I figure it oughta bring at least forty-five dollars. That includes harness for four horses, a spare wheel, and a tub of grease. We made him throw those in, though he didn't much want to."

What I knew about wagons wouldn't amount to much, but it sounded fair to me. When Nancy dug me in the ribs, I reached into my pocket, and came up with a pair of half eagles.

"Would you accept a ten-dollar deposit?" I asked him. "We couldn't take it with us today. Got a load of groceries for the ranch cook we have to haul out. Perhaps we can come by in a day or two, and give you the balance. We'll bring in a team, so we can take it on out to the ranch."

"Sure! A deposit will be just fine," he said. "I'm certain that you'll be pleased with the wagon. Since we're the agents for Studebaker, we know their product. There isn't a better rig made, anywhere. Here. Let me give you a receipt for that money." After he'd filled out the form, he handed it over, and we shook on it. I told him I appreciated his kindness.

"Thanks again, Mr. Wright. I will have the rest in a few days. Lot depends on me getting time away from the ranch."

"Please call me Bob," he said. "Most all my friends do." He turned to Nancy....

"Now, little missy, where's old Charley's grocery list? I better get one of the boys started on it. Knowing him, that list's bound to be longer'n one of Doc's war stories."

Opening her reticule, Nancy rummaged around and drew out the list.

"It's time I bought myself a new dress," she told him. "I think maybe I'll just go over there and look around. If you want to go have a beer, Case, you go right ahead. It'll take some time for the grocery order, and I'll be right here, if you need me."

"Believe I will," I replied. Turning back to Wright and unbuckling my gunbelt, I asked him if I might leave it there.

"Surest thing," he answered. "It'll be under the counter, up by the cash register. Nobody'll bother it there."

The Long Branch was just two doors down, and I managed to get in this time without meeting anyone with a black beard. The place was pretty full for a Monday morning, but I found a space near one end of the bar.

The bartender was the same man who'd waited on us before, and he came right over, a wide smile on his Irish face.

"Well! If it ain't the champeen o' greater Dodge City! I was hopin' you'd be back. The bosses figger your money's no good in this here bar. It's all on the house! So name your pleasure, and I'll trot it right on out."

I grinned at him. "What's all this horraw about, 'champeen'? All I done was protect myself from a drunk. We would never have tangled if he hadn't tried using his boots on me. I'd never cared much for being stomped. Man uses his feet on me once, he's got me to lick, and I don't much care how I get a deal like that done. Truth is, he couldn't have punched his way out of a wet feedsack, much less whipped a man his size. He was too drunk to know what was going on."

"That don't make no never mind," he retorted. "He caused trouble, every time he came into this place. We tried refusin' him service, but that just made him meaner. As a matter of fact..."

He turned toward a big fellow standing farther down the bar. "Hey! McCowan! You recollect that ugly black-bearded galoot you had problems with? Last year it was, about this same time of year. C'mere a minute. Got someone I want you to meet up with."

The man he called out to came slowly toward us. He was truly big! Almost seven feet tall, his massive arms and shoulders bulged under a thin canvas brush-jacket, and he was cat-haunched, with a chest like a silvertip grizzly. The mug he carried in one ham-sized hand looked not much bigger than a regular glass, while his wrists resembled hickory posts. Behind him trailed a smaller man.

"You wanted me, Sam?" he asked. His voice, though deeply pitched, was surprisingly gentle. His dark-hued face bore a terrible scar that began above his left ear and slanted almost to his chin. It was ropelike in texture, and starkly ivory against the mahogany skin. A hawkish nose jutted, like the blade of a tomahawk, down over a wide, generous-lipped mouth right now parted in an inquiring smile.

"Yeah! Want you to meet Case here. Case isn't really his name," he explained. "He got his head banged up a mite, and can't remember who he is right now.

"Case! This here's Lysander McCowan. Folks all call him 'Lightly,' and why, I don't know. As you can see, there's a whole lot of him."

With some apprehension, I let my hand be swallowed in his massive paw. To my relief, he exerted only the slightest of pressure. He held on for only a moment and continued smiling.

"Pleased to make your acquaintance," he said. "So you had trouble with our black-bearded friend, eh? Myself, I *had* to shut him up. He was bound to turn a spilled whiskey into a regular free-for-all. Tables and chairs cost money, and I'd no intention to pay for any in here. He was drunk, or close to it, and didn't seem at all concerned about the difference in our sizes. I just slapped him a couple of times and escorted him to the door. I figgered he'd be waiting outside later on, but wasn't no sign of him then or since. I reckoned he must have sobered up and had a change of heart, or mebbe didn't remember."

"I had the same thought," I told him. "As you said, he'd disappeared, when we left here. Actually, our little tangle wasn't much of a fight. Sort of one-sided, with me throwing all the punches. I'm sure not proud of what I did!"

"Proud?" It was Sam butting in.... "Who's sayin' anything about bein' proud? Shucks! It was the slickest job I ever did see! You shoulda been here, Lightly! Smash! Case hits him with his palm, and busts his nose. Pow! Right square in the old bread-basket. Then pow, again, right smackdab in the same place. Three punches throwed, and old Blackbeard taken a count of ten. Mister, he was all done! And he'd been the one who started it all. Caught Case here unawares, shoved him down on the walk, and tried to put the boots to him. We seen the last of that four-flusher, I'd bet on that."

"I hope you're right," said McCowan. "Feller like that is trouble for everybody, and I've had enough to last me a lifetime." He turned to me....

"What say we have another beer, and sit for a spell. I'd like to hear more about this 'lost memory' of yours." With one hand, he waved toward his companion who had been standing quietly by during our conversation.

"This here's Samuel Walker Wyeth. Sam's sorta my adopted brother. He's *segundo* on my place down south, and bosses a trail herd for us now and then. We've got one coming up now. It's about five, six days behind us, movin' slow, so's to not melt off any tallow."

Wyeth and I shook hands and he murmured a quiet greeting. A man about my age, he was of average height with pale blue eyes that met mine squarely. Was it my imagination, or some trick of the lighting? Seemed there had been a brief flicker of recognition before he dropped his gaze. Could it be that he recognized me as Frank Specter?

We sat down at a table in a corner and the bartender had our beer there in seconds. He stood there a moment, obviously wanting to be included, but another customer hollered for service and he had to leave.

"None of my business, but what's this about you

not knowing your own name? How did something like that come about?"

It was McCowan who asked the question. Sipping his beer, he looked at me over the top of the mug. His eyes were very dark, almost black, and his hair could have been pulled from a horse's mane. He looked very much like an Indian. I said as much, and he chuckled....

"I am," he admitted. "Paw was a full-blooded Choctaw. I take after him, even more'n my two brothers. He was a large man, like me, and stronger'n most. I'm purely proud of him, and just as proud to be thought of as an Indian."

"As well you have a right to be," I replied. "I've had a chance to learn more about them, just recently, and found my new friends were worth knowing."

I went on to tell them how I'd woke up alongside the railroad tracks, practically scalped, and how the Claytons, with their generosity, had helped me to survive.

"They are great folks, and I thank whatever gods there be for their kindness to me."

We sat there and talked for a while. Then Mc-Cowan hauled out his watch and glanced at the face. He frowned....

"I'd best git over and see that buyer," he said. "Hate to leave good company, but business comes first. You comin' along, Sam?"

Wyeth looked up for a moment. His mug still held a measure of beer. He shook his head.

"Nah! You go on ahead, and I'll ketch up later. I ain't rode sixty miles jest to listen to you argue price with the cattle buyers. I'm gonna finish this here beer, and I might jest have another. *Vayale!* Don't you worry none about me."

The big man stood after we'd shaken hands again. "Wishin' you the best of luck," he told me. "Myself,

I don't get around this town more'n once a year, but if you're ever down around our neck of the woods, be sure and come see us. We'd be pleased to see you, my wife and I. *Adios y hasta luego.*"

"In case you don't savvy the lingo," said Sam, "he wished you God's protection, until you meet again." He finished his beer and held up his hand for a refill.

"Care for another?" he asked me, reaching into his pocket for some change.

As we sat there, he filled me in on the McCowan family, a mother and three sons who had come originally from Kentucky. Then he faced me squarely and his voice hardened slightly.

"Mister," he said. "I don't know nothin' about folks not knowin' who they are. I've heard stories, but never did see anyone like that up close.

"Now, I *know* who you are, and what you've done, so if you *are* playin' a game, jest you tell me so!" Slowly, his right hand had slid from the table, and dropped by his side.

My breath caught in my throat! He knew! What could I do now? Suddenly, I realized how much I stood to lose. How my whole world would fall apart if Nancy was lost to me. What I had told myself was only friendship was a love so strong I couldn't bear losing any part of it!

I was building a brand new life! What a lousy hand that fate decided to deal me. Nancy! Judah! All of my friends! All gone now. Gone because some two-bit, stringbean Texan, a man I'd never seen before, was going to tell them about my forgotten past. My fists clenched, I glared across at him.

Wyeth had been watching me intently. His eyes narrowed, then he leaned forward and spoke softly....

"I didn't see you packin' iron, but I gotta warn

yuh. My hand's on a forty-four Colt, stuck down in my boot. I can put lead into you, if you even blink!"

"Don't worry none," I gritted out bitterly. "Just speak your piece, and tell me who I am. I'm not armed, so you can quit worrying about that. Come on, damn you! Spit it out!"

He looked at me in surprise. "You're tellin' the truth!" He raised his hand back onto the table and shook his head.

"I really thought you was runnin' some sort of sandy, but you don't know, do you? That hit on the head. It did something that scrambled your brains. You're not puttin' on!"

"No," I told him. "I'm not 'putting on,' as you thought. But I was shown a newspaper recently that gave me some idea who I might be, and I'm not too happy finding that out. You apparently know who I am, so please tell me. I'm okay now."

"About ten years ago, I was in Jacksboro, Texas. I saw a shoot-out between you and two troopers out of Fort Richardson. They laid for you. Tried to ketch you in a cross fire, with no chance of you gittin' 'em both. But you did! You killed one with two shots in the heart. They were so close together, it looked more like one big hole.

"The other feller wound up with a smashed shoulder, and I couldn't figger at the time why you didn't kill him too. A moment there, I thought you was gonna, but you holstered the gun and jest walked on outta there. That was something! I never in my borned days seen a man git to shootin' so fast! Them three shots sounded more like jest one. Them black men never knew what hit 'em!"

"I read all about it," I told him wearily. "Why wasn't I arrested? Can you tell me that?"

"Bet I can! You went on outta there like a striped

cat! Big sorrel horse, with two white socks in the back. Fast as greased lightning, that horse. Wasn't a pony in that posse, could even come close. Yessir, Joe. You got away clean."

It took a minute for what he'd said to penetrate. He had called me "Joe." What did he mean? I was Frank Specter!

"Say that again," I told him. "You called me Joe. Who's Joe? Why did you call me that?"

"Why?" he sounded indignant. "'Cause that's your name! I saw you then, and I see you now. Joe Warner. W-a-r-n-e-r."

CHAPTER TEN

FOR A BRIEF moment, I felt a tremendous relief. This man didn't know me at all, and couldn't expose me as the killer Frank Specter. I was still safe in my new identity. He was mistaken, and thought me to be someone else....

My head was whirling! The story of the two black troopers matched the one in *Harper's* to a tee. Flashes of sweat-streaked black faces and rumpled, dusty uniforms appeared and disappeared in my mind. A barroom...a table overturned and lying on its side...a splintered chair...broken glass glittering in the yellow lantern light...faces loomed at me, grossly out of proportion...eyes stared accusingly and arms clutched, fingers tearing at my clothes...a voice shrieked..."They're dead! He's getting away! Stop him!"

Now I *was* confused....It didn't make any sense, but he'd sounded so positive. Joe Warner! Who'n hell was Joe Warner, and what connection did he have with Frank Specter? I tried to compose myself and think logically, but none of it would make any sense. Could it be that Joe Warner and Frank Specter were one and the same man? I collected my wits, staring across the table at Sam Wyeth.

"Honest," I told him. "I've never heard that name before today. Ten years ago...How can you be so sure?"

"Ought to know it. I've seen enough posters out for you. Not for a long time, though. Just for the first three years or so, then they quite puttin' 'em up. There for a time, the Army brass made a big fuss, them two bein' soldiers and all, so your bounty jumped to a hundred dollars, dead or alive.

"Hey! Don't look so worried! I wouldn't have tried collecting then, and I sure won't now. Had that comin' to 'em, jumpin' you like that. Never did find out why they did it."

Wyeth was watching me closely and appeared concerned by my reaction. He scratched his head.... "Look," he said. "I had you figgered for runnin' some sorta humbug game on these folks around here. I can see now that I read your sign all wrong. Beginnin' right now, I never did hear of Joe Warner, and I couldn't pick him outta a war party of Comanches."

I considered him for a moment....I couldn't go on worrying every time a strange face turned up. I had to confide in someone.

"Wyeth," I asked. "Who are you? What's your stake in my affairs? One minute you're after my scalp, and now you say that you're on my side. I can't figure you out, I swear."

Slowly his big grin faded, and his face took on a serious cast. He finished his beer in one long swallow, set the mug down on the table, and wiped his face with his sleeve.

"Mister! I know what it feels like to be all alone, with sorrow ridin' on one shoulder, uncertainty on the other, and old Death settin' right solid in the middle of your back. I was jest twelve years old when my ma and pa died, leavin' a scared boy out in the middle of west Texas, with nothin' but a blanket, a spavined, rib-sprung old horse, and a length of rope for a Comanche war bridle.

"Old Death had his arm around my neck, and one hand in my pocket, when the McCowan boys found me lost in the brush. I never figgered there was another human bein' in a hundred or more miles, and I'd given up ever eatin' or drinkin' again.

"Them McCowans taken me in, and treated me like I was one of their own! Missus McCowan put her arms around me, hugged me with tears in her eyes, and called me son. I've tried to live up to that word. To be as fair and square, as honest a man, as her real sons have always been. I've never broken a promise, or gone back on my word, and I've tried to give all men at least one chance." He shoved back his chair and got to his feet. The grin came back and he offered his hand....

"That's 'bout all I got to say. I wish you the best, and like Lysander said, the latchstring's out, if you're ever in our part of Texas. Place called Juno, in the Val Verde."

I watched him leave, then told the bartender I'd be back one day soon and went out into the street myself. Traffic had thinned out some, and across the way a man was throwing pails of water on the dusty thoroughfare. He looked up and waved when he saw me standing there.

"Hello, Champ! How you feeling today? Come by any time you're in town. Dinner's on the house."

I waved back. "Yeah! Thanks a lot!" I answered in kind.

His place of business was a small eatery of some kind or other. I suppose he was another victim of Blackbeard's.

Glancing into Wright and Beverly's, I could see that Nancy was finished with her shopping. She was standing up by the front counter, deep in conversation with Bob Wright. One of the young clerks was coming out, trundling a wheelbarrow full of sacks and boxes. We loaded them into the wagon, as another boy brought out a second barrow full.

Altogether, there were nine loads of goods, and they did a pretty good job of filling the wagon. I was happy to see the last box, and tipped the boys a nickel each.

Nancy looked up as I walked in to the store. She took a large package off the counter and handed it to me.

"I was about to send out a scout," she teased. "Thought maybe you had gotten lost in the big city."

Bob Wright reached behind the counter and brought out a box with my gunbelt inside. He handed me the rig, and then watched with interest as I buckled it around my waist.

"I can remember the early days, here in Dodge, when every man in town wore one of those, or carried a rifle. We never knew what to expect, from one day to the next.

"Injuns were always a problem, but mostly it was trouble, and of our own making. During the buffalo days, the hunters and skinners used to hit here, with their pockets plumb full of money, and them hell bent to spend it all. Didn't take a whole lot of time for them to get that done.

"Usually, it was a bath and haircut first, followed by an outfit of new clothes, from the skin on out. Then they'd go in to the nearest saloon, and try their darndest to drink all the whiskey in the place. Fights would start, on the slightest pretext, and sometimes the best of friends would maim or kill each other.

"Toward the last, when their money was about gone, and a headache was all they had to show for six months hard labor, they would look around for a scapegoat. Someone they could blame for all their excesses. The shopkeepers, the saloons, even the painted ladies on whom they'd lavished gifts.

"That's when they'd decide to wreck the town, burn everything to the ground, wipe out the cheats and shylocks who'd victimized them. What they seldom considered was that most of us had cut our teeth on guns. Many townsmen were veterans from the War of the Rebellion, and had seen years of combat. Some had an enviable record as sharpshooters. All were men who had come to the frontier knowing the risks and dangers involved, and prepared to cope with them.

"So instead of pantywaisted clerks, they found themselves confronted by determined men, who were not about to knuckle under to a bunch of hungover ruffians. That first year, we buried twenty-five victims of knife and gunshot wounds. The population of Dodge then, eighteen seventy-two, was only about five hundred. That's a rather high percentage of violent deaths.

"After a time, we hired a marshal to keep the peace here, and that made it possible for us to put away our guns. However, you'll find that even today, in these modern times, no citizen in Dodge lets his guns rust or go uncleaned. Conditions and town may change, but people remain the same.

"Well!" he chuckled. "That was quite a speech! I was reminded, seeing you with that rig."

Nancy reached over and gave him a hug. "We better be on our way, Uncle Bob. Old Charley's always hard to handle if we're the least bit late with his groceries. You'd think we were down to our last crust of dry bread, the way he carries on. Thanks again for letting Case buy that wagon at a bargain price! I'll try to get in and see you real soon."

Wright and I shook hands, and he hung on a moment, giving me a thorough appraisal. He apparently approved of what his scrutiny had observed, because he grinned and grasped me by the shoulder.

"Young man, it's been a real pleasure meeting you, and we hope you have decided to become a permanent member of Kansas society, preferably here in Ford County. We all think a lot of our little girl, here, and we're pretty choosey about who pays court to her. I don't know much about you, but I'd say that you'll do!"

Nancy blushed and grabbed me by the hand. "Shame on you, Uncle Bob. You've embarrassed me! What will he think of us now? C'mon, Case! Take this package, and let's get going."

She handed me the wrapped bundle and we went outside. I handed her up into the wagon and put the package behind the seat. As we pulled away from the storefront, Bob Wright was standing in the doorway, waving goodbye.

My emotions were mixed. Wright's words, delivered so sincerely, had touched me where it hurt. No matter my feelings.... The fact remained that I was traveling under false pretenses. I was not the clean-cut young man he presumed me to be. Not a man I'd want my daughter in love with, I said to myself. No! I was Frank Specter, or Joe Warner, or perhaps both. Killer for hire! A gunfighter who could kill another man as easily as he would step on an insect.

The westbound train was stopped at the station, and rigs were loading passengers and baggage. As we drove down Front Street, a buckboard was just pulling out with a middle-aged couple and a girl of perhaps Nancy's age. She waved at us, and Nancy asked me to pull the wagon over near them. I did, and we stopped alongside, where Nancy and the girl exchanged greetings and I was introduced to Mr. and Mrs. Tom Rollins and their daughter Frances. Mrs. Rollins had just returned from a trip to Kansas City where she'd visited her mother.

I listened in amazement as Nancy told them how I planned to go into the cattle business soon, and had decided that my ranch would be located somewhere in Ford County.

"Will we see you two at the dance Saturday night?" asked Frances. "They expect a real big turnout, what with racing and some other sports events, earlier in the day. You won't disappoint us, will you Nance? Everybody's gonna be there."

"Why! 'Course not!" Nancy replied. 'We'd naturally planned to attend. Wouldn't miss it for the world, would we?"

She turned to me, and a steely glint in her eyes belied her big smile. I nodded, vigorously, and almost shouted.

"That's right," I said. "We've been planning on it, over a week now. Saturday just ain't Saturday, without a dance."

"I'll save you a dance on my card, Case," Frances told me. "That is, I'll put you down, if you want me to." A friendly girl, she was tall and almost painfully thin. Her parents, who were courteous enough, seemed in a hurry to leave, and I could understand why. Mrs. Rollins had been away from home, and was anxious to return. Another round of handshakes, and we were once more on our way.

I drove along in silence for ten minutes or more, and the girl beside me was equally quiet. When I'd finally decided, I turned to speak, and we both burst out at the same time....

"You go ahead," I told her. "You speak first."

"No!" she said. "It's your turn. I've done enough talking for one day."

"Well, I agree on that, missy. What on earth ever possessed you to tell those folks I was planning on a ranch? What was your reason for telling a deliberate falsehood? Why you could have knocked me down with a broomstraw! I didn't know what to say, when you told them that big fib."

She looked at me defiantly. "Well! Don't you plan having a ranch of your own, some day? Are you gonna go on working for someone else for the rest of your life?"

"Well, yes...er, uh...no....No, I ain't gonna cowboy for someone else all my life. Sure! Sure I want a place of my own, some day. Who doesn't?"

She wouldn't let up, and now she pressed her advantage....

"All right," she said smugly. "Then you *have* planned the ranch, and I didn't tell any such falsehood. You know," she went on. "We just had our first quarrel. I hope we'll have no reason to ever quarrel again, don't you?"

"Gosh, no!" I hastened to reassure her. "I mean, yes! I mean, I don't want to ever fuss with you, Nancy." The humor in what I had just stammered started filtering through, and I chuckled....Then the chuckle turned into a laugh and, unable to stop myself, I roared! Nancy's frown dissolved into a hesitant smile. She shook her head in wonderment, and giggled, A moment later, a wild shriek of laughter burst forth, and she was as helpless as I had become....

I brought the team to a halt and, with an effort, brought my laughter under control. Nancy, by this time, had her arm around my neck and her head buried on my shoulder. She was reduced to hiccups and giggles, and her back was quivering.

Wrapping the lines around the brake lever, I embraced her with one arm and patted her tenderly with my other hand. A giggle became a sigh, and she raised her tear-streaked face. Her full lips were slightly parted, and her eyes stared into mine, her brows lifted expectantly....

We kissed....Just a touch, at first, then drawing apart. An indrawn breath...her eyes shining, the deep blue flecked with sparks of gold. Then once more our lips touched, my heart pounding, and I strained to hold her close.

After a long moment, we drew apart, but continued to hold each other's arms. My heart was still going like a trip-hammer, and I could feel a hot flush on my cheeks. Nancy's hat was askew, and her curls were down over one eye. She drew a deep breath and gasped....

"Whew! That's a lot of work!" She looked at me saucily, her head cocked over to one side. "But it was sure worth it! I'd been wondering when we'd get around to doing that. I've wanted to kiss you, Case. Last night, I came close to flinging myself in your arms, but I settled for that peck on your cheek. I'm in love with you, Case. I guess you know that."

I drew her close, and laid her head on my shoulder. Just wanted to holler out loud, I was so happy! This lovely girl had just confessed her love for me, and shown that she needed me to love her in return. What more could I ask?

Then the reality of my position gave me reason for second thoughts. With the grim threats of Frank Specter's past now so close to being unveiled, what did I have to offer? Money perhaps, because a man in Specter's line would be well paid. Of that, I was fairly certain. But could I ever give her my assurance that I would remain alive from day to day? Guarantee her the security and stability of a normal marriage?

But how about Bill Tilghman? His life as a peace officer obviously carried a certain amount of risk. He was married, and had been for six years. He'd told me that only yesterday, and from his tone, theirs was a successful marriage.

Perhaps there was a chance for us after all. From Bill I had gotten the impression that Specter's gunfights were at least on the side of the law. With the exception of the one in Jacksboro, that is, and that had been ten years ago. The Army, it seemed, wasn't trying to prosecute him at this late date. With Specter so much in the public eye, it would have been simple to arrest him at any time. I made up my mind....

Nancy pulled away and sat up straight on the wagon seat. Looking away, she tugged at her dress, and tucked the strayed curls up under her bonnet with shaking hands.

"Did I talk out of turn, Case?" she asked me. "Is this a one-sided romance, or do you feel the same way about me?"

Taking her hands in mine, I shook her, gently. She turned, and looked into my eyes....

"What do you see, girl? Isn't my love for you showing on my face, for all the world to see? Of course I love you! I guess I've loved you from that very first day. I've dreamed of you, and imagined how wonderful it would be if we had a place of our own, and could be together, in our love.

"But think for a moment! Consider how little I have to offer. I'm not even certain who I am, nor what I might have been, in that past I can't recall. This life, the one we're living now, began the day we met.

"Here's all I ask of you. Give me some time to adjust my thoughts. If not to remember the past, at least to build up something for our future. Right now, we can't afford any of the things needed for a marriage. That will change! Remember only that I do love you. Love you with all my heart!"

She leaned forward, her arms going around my neck, and my resolves were forgotten for a long moment. We kissed again, and held each other tightly. This time, it was a more practical Nancy who gently disengaged.

"Don't believe I could stand more'n two dollars worth of that," she giggled. "An old joke, Case. Remind me, and I'll tell you some day."

Then, more seriously, she went on. "I will remember, dearest. It's going to be hard to keep this secret. Right now, I want the whole world to know, and especially my dad. He'd be so happy, I know. He's worried so that I never would meet a man that I could love and respect as I do my father. I'm twenty-one, you know, and that's practically an old maid here in Kansas. So, whip up those mules, and let's get going!"

As I got the wagon started back down the road again, some questions came to mind, and one of them had to do with cash and a wagon in Dodge that had to be paid for.

"Now that we're alone," I said, "tell me what you had in mind, when you insisted we buy that wagon from Bob Wright."

"Why, that's easy," she told me. "The Indian couple! We were wondering what to do with them, and you said it'd be so much easier, if they were in Montana. Well...Now they can travel to Montana in style. With the proper clothing, and a bit of luck, they'll do just fine!"

I was impressed! But there was still the matter

of thirty-five bucks, and how I could manage to pay it. Payday was two weeks away, and I'd promised to bring in the balance before the end of the week. I said as much to Nancy, and then watched as she dug down in her reticule.

"Here!" she chortled. "Hold out your hand."

From a small buckskin sack, she counted out seven coins, all bright, shiny half eagles. I didn't know what to say....

"Don't worry," she said with a grin. "They're honest. I started saving these when I was a little girl. I got more. Enough to buy a hundred wagons like that one. So we aren't exactly broke, you see. You're marrying a girl with a dowry to boot. Don't worry," she hastened to add. "I know you want the where-with-all to do it right, and I agree. This is just an ace in the hole, in case we ever need it."

I nodded and stuffed the coins in my pocket. We were on the last leg of the military road, and ahead of us I saw the turnoff to the ranch. Our visit to Dodge City had certainly been an interesting and exciting one. It had brought things out into the open between Nancy and me, and I'd learned all about Joe Warner. Meeting McCowan had impressed me, even if we never laid eyes on each other again, and I felt in Wyeth I had a friend I could trust. If we ever did get down Texas way, we would look him up.

As we neared the turn, Nancy grabbed my arm and pointed. Perhaps fifty yards off the road, a dog coyote was trotting, his tail all bushed out in pride and a jackrabbit dangling from his mouth. I reckoned he was headed for home, with his hunt a successful one....

CHAPTER ELEVEN

It wasn't until I'd carried in the last box of groceries, then helped Charley Fong store them away in his pantry, that I remembered the chestnut gelding in the corral. Apparently Nancy had also forgotten, because she said something about a nap and went off to her room.

Charley poured me a cup of coffee and set out a wedge of rhubarb pie big as a saddle blanket. I didn't have any way to save part of it, so I ate the whole darn piece. It sure tasted good. Right down to the last crumb.

After I'd changed into jeans and chaps, I went on down to the corral and took a look at the gelding. He was a really fine-looking horse. Not overly big, he stood maybe a trifle over fifteen hands, and would weigh a bit more'n eleven hundred pounds. Almost a pure brown, his mane and tail were a bit lighter, and very long.

Patches of light hair showed where saddles had left gall marks on his hide. His feet were bare, but I could see nail holes on the edges of his hoofs. He'd cast his shoes, and I figured it hadn't been too long ago. Possibly he'd run away from a trail herd, but I couldn't imagine them not trying to run him down. No. I'd almost be willing to bet that somewhere behind this horse, a dead man was lying, unburied. In the remains of his camp at the bottom of an arroyo, or down behind some rocks, an empty pistol by his hand.

The chestnut was still wearing a braided hair hackamore, with perhaps two feet of tattered picket line attached. Had he fought that line for days, hungry and thirsty and panic-stricken, because his rider lay dead and couldn't free him? No one would ever know, I reckoned.

Well, enough philosophy for one day. Time to get the job done. I brought my saddle out of the shed and racked it on the corral rails. No bridle, because I'd decided to use the hackamore. It was possible he'd never had a bit in his tender mouth, and I didn't want to add to my problems.

I slipped through the rails and approached him, building a loop in my rope. "Huh, horse. Easy now, boy. E-a-s-y...Like the old man said...this is gonna hurt me, more'n you. Whoa, now...There!" I'd slipped the loop over his head, a throw not being necessary.

Careful not to excite him, I led him around the corral a couple of times, talking to him and telling him what a fine horse he was. Several times he started to jerk away, but I held him firmly, with the rope doubling back over the hondo so the noose couldn't tighten and choke him. Gradually, we were getting a little better acquainted, and he almost acted as if he was enjoying the parade. Time for the second phase of his training.

After tying him to a lower rail, near the saddle, I showed him the blanket. Let him smell it and make sure nothing could hurt him. I passed it over most of his body, careful that it didn't flap or make a sound that would frighten him. After ten minutes or so, he seemed to have gotten accustomed to it, so I laid the blanket over his back and leaned my weight on him.

He tried to sidestep, but the rope brought him up with an anguished squeal. I stepped back, crooning to him.... "Easy horse...Easy, boy...Not gonna hurt you...." The blanket, wet from the horse's sweat, had stayed in place.

I loosed the rope off the rail and walked him around the corral a few more times, the blanket on his back. At intervals I stopped and put my arm over his back, allowing some of my weight to be felt. After a while, he accepted this as part of the game, and stood there quietly. It was time.

The saddle was heavy, and had things like stirrups, cinch, and saddle ties hanging from it. It was important that none of these rattled, or flopped around. He could panic and undo all we'd accomplished so far, if he was frightened.

After tying him back on the rail, I carefully lifted that saddle over his back and lowered it into place. He humped, but he stood still, and didn't try to fight the rope. I had hooked the off stirrup over the horn, to keep it from moving around, and now I let it down together with the cinch. The horse was quivering slightly, but his feet stayed in place.

Gingerly, I reached under his belly and pulled the cinch toward me, passing the latigo through the ring. Three doubling passes and I drew the cinch up tight, securing it with a hitch.

"Whew!" I told him. "I'm glad we got that done so easy!" Still talking to him, I got out the makings and rolled me a smoke. Once more, I untied the rope, and we walked around.

Again, I paused several times and leaned some

of my dead weight over the saddle. He didn't seem to mind a bit. When I'd finished my smoke, I pinched out the butt and dropped it on the ground. Reckoned I'd stalled long enough.

In my chap pocket, I had about six feet of soft cotton rope about an inch in diameter. I cut off the fragment remaining from the picket line, and fastened my cotton lead in its place. Drawing on buckskin gloves, I ran my eye around the corral. Circular in shape, it had no square corners to get caught in, but the snubbing post in the center could be a hazard. I'd have to watch out for it.

"Well, horse, reckon it's about that time. Let's make it short and sweet. You go ahead and buck to your heart's content, cause it's the last time you'll do it with me on your back." Gathering the improvised bronc rein and one side of the hackamore in my left fist, I pulled the chestnut's head around and stepped up into the saddle....

With a surprised grunt, the horse shied away from the corral fence, half rearing and spinning to the right. Then he systematically set out to dislodge me. All four feet left the ground until he hung like an inverted horseshoe, then a spin to the left as he came down. Reversing, he'd hump into the air and spin to the right. I lost a stirrup and bit my tongue on about the fourth bone-jarring bounce, and lost my seat in the saddle on the fifth.

The rein was wrapped around my fist, and him being on the move, I was stretched out and landed full length. I stayed there for a while, trying to decide if getting up was what I wanted to do. Darned if he didn't come over to me and nuzzle at my head, whickering all the while.

I sat up and stared at him, and he turned his head away, pawing at the dirt and making a stuttering, grunting sound, deep in his throat. Almost like he was saying, "Sure sorry, but I warned you not to climb up on my back."

This time I was forced to make an express rider's mount, as he was side-stepping away faster than I could hop. That there were no witnesses to this exhibition gave me some degree of comfort, but didn't make it any easier to bear.

Finally, I was locked back into the saddle, and he settled down to some real old-fashioned bucking. He soon tired of that, and decided to sunfish. Up in the air he'd soar...until he topped out, twisting wickedly, in an attempt to turn his belly to the sun. My nose started to bleed, adding to the stream from my gashed tongue, and my vision was starting to blur.

Suddenly he stopped! Just flat quit, and stood there for a moment, his breathing ragged and his sides working like a bellows. A sound, like an agonized moan, came from way down in his chest, and he made a few halfhearted crow hops, his feet close together. Then he quit again, his head down and his hide covered with lather.

I slid off and loosened the cinch. "Easy now, boy. You did a fine job, but now it's all over, and we're both tired. We'll just cool you off a bit."

I rolled a smoke, lit it, and started leading him around, all the time talking to him and telling him what a fine old fellow he was and how he didn't have to prove anything now. I was pretty tired myself, and my neck felt like someone had smacked me with an axe handle. My chin and the front of my shirt were bloody, and my ears rang like a dinner bell.

There were two big box stalls in the barn, and I decided to put him in one of them, but first I had to try something. His breathing had become much easier, so I drew the cinch up tight and climbed back into the saddle. Leaning forward, I checked the bridge of his nose for cuts or bruising, finding it undamaged. The *bosal* of the hackamore was a hard, plaited leather band that fitted over the horse's nose; and firm pressure on the reins would be painfully felt on that tender part of the horse's anatomy.

Touching my blunt spurs to his flanks, I rode over to the corral gate and, bending down, opened it wide. Once outside the corral, he began to take a renewed interest in his surroundings. I put him into an easy lope, and we made for the small pasture where Nancy kept the milk cow. I had noticed a line of posts still remaining from a previously fenced-in area. The wire had been taken down.

The first time, I put him through at a walk, threading in and out of the posts which were about ten feet apart. Then I increased the pace, spurring him into a swinging lope. To my delight, he made it without so much as brushing a post.

Now came the true test! Starting perhaps fifty feet away from the line, I spurred him into a flat-out run. The posts flashed by in a blur, as we weaved between them without any mishap. All this done without touching the rein. My knees had given the commands! What a great cowhorse he would make me! I leaned forward and patted him on the neck.

"Good boy! You did just fine! For that, you get..."

"No matter what he gets," a familiar voice broke in, "you deserve that, and much more." It was Judah. Beside him, on a big steeldust gelding, was Bud Larkin, the ranch foreman.

"Where'd you ever learn to break horses?" he asked. "Oh! I forgot! Sorry, Case, my mind's not like it used to be. I gotta give you a pat on the back, though. Buck and another one of the boys got throwed off that horse time after time, and finally gave up. How'd you do it?"

"Well, Bud, it didn't come easy." I pointed to the dried blood on my shirt front. "Wasn't really a matter of breaking him, because the marks showed he'd been ridden. Mainly, the horse had been badly scared, and apparently blamed it on all humans. Really, all I did was prove that I could stay up on top without hurting him. He's a fine horse, as you can see by what he just performed. I'd like to buy him from you, if you could see your way clear, Judah. You could take it from my pay, until your price was met."

"Ain't my horse, Case. He's a stray, and without a brand on him, there ain't no way we can find his owner. I'll talk to the boys, 'cause they found him and brought him in, but I don't think they'll begrudge you the horse."

Well, this had turned into quite a day for me. First, my meeting with McCowan, and Sam Wyeth who had told me about a man named Joe Warner. Then Nancy, that lovely girl I had no idea could care for me, confessed her love and her longing. Perhaps even more important was the concession I'd reached with myself, as to whether or not professional gunmen should consider marriage.

I thanked Judah, and told him I'd see them both at supper. "Right now, I'm going to give this old boy his reward. He's earned a good rubdown, and some oats. Tomorrow, if you have no objections, I'd like to try him out on some cattle."

He nodded. "Better still, I'll find some cuttin' job on the graze. One that has to be done anyway. By the way, we brought them bulls in, from over on the Pawnee. They're out in the big stock pen. You might take a look at 'em, if your new cuttin' horse'll spare you the time." He laughed....

I walked my horse around for a spell, cooling him out. A thorough rubbing came next, paying special attention to legs and shoulders. I threw an old blanket over him and cinched it with a surcingle, then took him to water where I allowed him to drink sparingly.

Back in the barn, I forked fresh straw into a stall, then filled the rack with sweet prairie hay, and turned him loose with two quarts of oats. Affectionately, he slammed me into the partition with his shoulder, and started gobbling grain, blowing through his nostrils as the husks floated up.

"Yore gonna spoil that pony, feedin' him so rich!" Maw's voice echoed in my ears.... "Fu'st thing y'know, his feet'll be bigger'n pie plates, and he'd have him a case of founder a body can't cure. Yore paw'll have to shoot him! You want that, Joe? Would you ruther *walk* to school?"

Joe? The voice had sounded so real! It *was* my mother's familiar tones, ringing so clearly in my head. An image had appeared, the figure blurred and indistinct but clearly one of a woman in a brown dress, her face framed in black hair.

Then we were in a kitchen...a familiar room, where we'd taken our meals after Paw said the blessing....Paw! But I am older, now! I'm twenty-five years old, and I have to get away from here! I just stopped to get a fresh horse....

"Happened so quick, Paw! It was me or them, and they had me in a cross fire. I *had* to shoot, Paw!" His face was saddened, and he looked so old. There was a worn clasp purse, open in his hands, and he was pressing a gold piece in mine.

"It's all I got, son. There's money in the bank, but you don't dare go to town. You take care now, y'hear? We..."

The images faded and I was back in the box stall. I remembered now. I *was* Joe Warner! I'd lived on a ranch, just a few miles out of Jacksboro. It wasn't a big place, a half section my folks had proved up, after we moved there from a farm in Virginia. My father ran his beef on leased grass.

I'd killed one soldier and wounded another. They'd been angry when I'd turned down their request for money. I told them to go back to the fort and sober up, and not to do any begging while they were wearing an Army uniform. Straighten up, I'd said, and don't disgrace yourselves—and the Army.

There had been three of them, with guns in their hands. I was sitting at a table, talking with Arnie...Arnie Baca! Another name from the past! They came at me from different directions. One of them hollered something....

I fell trying to get out of the chair, and somehow those first shots missed. My gun was in my hand, and I fired four times. The bigger man fell first, and his shoulder was covered with blood. Two bullets hit another, both shots striking his heart; the two holes, as one. The third man fled!

Arnie said something like "good shooting," and other men crowded up to shake my hand. The wounded man was making the most god-awful sounds, and screaming that the Army'd hang me for shooting soldiers. Everybody got sorta quiet, and someone said I'd best get on outta there, before the Army came....

The memory of riding my horse out to the ranch, and nearly killing him in the process; that was clear enough. But I couldn't remember leaving there, with a fresh horse under me. I tried hard, but it was just a blank.

There was no doubt in my mind that I was Joe Warner. Now the business about Frank Specter had me puzzled. That newspaper story had pointed out that Specter's career began when he killed one soldier and wounded his companion. This was too much of a coincidence, especially when the sketch in *Harper's* was considered. It was too close a likeness. A "spittin' image," Tilghman had said. Of me, when I was angered. Well, I couldn't get it sorted out right now, but if this piece of memory had come back, maybe more would in its own time. Meanwhile, I'd had enough for one day. But I was wrong about that.

Supper that night was a festive one. Nancy fairly well sparkled, and all Judah could talk about was his new bulls. I came in for some good natured ribbing, of course, and Buck was the leader there.

"C'mon, Case," he said. "Tell the truth. You poured the horse full of Charley Fong's lemon extract, and got him pie-eyed. I heard he was so drunk a cougar coulda rode him all the way to Dodge and back. He was out on his feet when old Bud and Judah come upon you, and they're willin' to swear to that!"

"T'ain't true, Buck," I retored. "Truth is, he threw me off several times, and I never would have ridden him, if I'd not scared him half to death."

"Oh! How'd you manage to do that?" he asked.

"Well, I rummaged around in the bunkhouse, and found that picture you had taken in St. Joe. The one with a fancy vest, and those hairy angora chaps. I let that horse see it, and told him I was gonna have it tattooed on his flank. He tamed right down, and practically begged me to try again. When I got on that time, he just walked off pretty as you please. Matter of fact, it was his idea to run those posts, so's I'd know he meant well."

That brought a laugh at Buck's expense, but he laughed as loud as the rest. A moment later, he had another tall tale, and the butt of his humor was a cowboy called Sim.

After the table was cleared, Judah and Bud both got tally books out and thumbed through the pages.

The foreman spoke first, as the schedule for the next day was outlined.

"Clemens, I want you to take your rifle, and scout around the high pasture, where we got those young heifers. I heard tell there's a stray range bull hangin' around, and I'd like to hear he dropped dead from a case of lead poisonin'. The last thing we want is calico longhorn mixed in with our own white-face stock. Besides, he's a runt. If you see him, be sure and kill him! He's your responsibility.

"Laidley, you and Sim will be ridin' fence. Take a packhorse, and load on a couple rolls of bobbed wire. Buck here says he seen some places along the north boundary, could use some patchin'. Figger on scoutin' the whole perimeter fence, and that'll hold you 'til fall. Oh, yeah! Better check out the line camps too. We'll be using 'em this winter. If you find any that ain't weathertight, you know where we keep the lumber and nails."

Judah broke in.... "Feller that held down the Injun Butte camp, last year, complained the rats stole all his grub. We don't want stories like that goin' 'round. Take a half dozen traps along, and drop 'em off there. Might even set a few."

Bud continued.... "Buck, you and Case here will give me'n Judah a hand with them new bulls. All gotta be branded, and we figger to use that squeezer chute to do it. Old Case can try out his new cuttin' horse. See if he's worth his salt."

"One more thing..." It was Judah who interrupted again, face set like a stone. "Me'n Bud ran into Cash Hollister, at Hodgeman's ranch. Cash is the deputy U.S. marshal from down around Caldwell. Seem's we got us a bad Injun wanderin' in these parts. Kiowa, named White Wolf, and his squaw. Squaw was foolin' around with a trader, at the Red River agency, a feller named Goldman.

White Wolf caught 'em, and killed the trader. Broke his back, and left him to die like an animal."

I swallowed the angry protest that came immediately. My worst fears were realized as Judah went on....

"Keep an eye peeled for this feller. Hollister says that he's dangerous. Used to be with the Agency police, and he's a dead shot. Don't waste words on him. Just kill the son!"

"What about the woman, boss?" It was Sim who asked that question. A man of about thirty-five, Simpkins, or Sim, was the one hand I'd not much liked during my stay at the ranch. He had a sly look about him, like he knew some secrets that he'd never share. He hung close to the foreman, and quickly agreed with him no matter what the subject. A short, stockily built man, he was enormously strong. I'd watched as he carried two rolls of barbed wire, one in each hand. Each of those rolls weighed over two hundred pounds.

Judah seemed irritated by the query, but he answered without any hesitation.

"The woman is not to be harmed, of course. If at all possible, she'll be brought here, and Hollister will be notified. It'll be up to him to decide what happens to her. Now I mean that! Unless she wants to fight, nobody tries to lay a hand on her! Is that understood?

"Well, that's about all I got to say. Might be better if you boys turn in early, tonight. We all got a big day ahead of us, and I want to see you bright-eyed and bushy-tailed in the mornin'!"

Nancy caught my eye as I rose with my plate and utensils in hand. I nodded, and went on out into the kitchen. A few moments later she followed, her arms loaded down with china. I helped her stack them in the sink, and she whispered in my ear as we leaned down.

"We have to talk! Ask me to go down to the pens with you. Say you want to look at the bulls, or something."

A few minutes later, I did just that, and Nancy agreed. I filled our cups with coffee, and went out the back to wait. Standing there on the porch, I lit a cigarette and began to think about the flashback I'd experienced in the barn. That I was, or had been, Joe Warner was unquestionably true. It was time for me to tell Nancy. Tell her what I knew must be truth, and also what I suspected. To wait any longer would be foolish and make it that much worse when the story came out. Especially if she were to hear it from someone else.

The screen door opened and Nancy came through. I gave her a cup, and we stood there and finished the coffee without a word being exchanged. A ray from the setting sun moved past a corner pillar and reflected off her wealth of sandy hair, creating an aura of flame around her face. She was lovelier than any angel, and she'd promised to be my wife. The story I was about to tell might cause her to turn away and never want to see me again, but I had to take that chance. It was something I had to do.

She took my arm as we started across the ranch yard, waving at her father who sat on the front porch with Bud. The sun was just a red line on the horizon, and as we watched, a faraway hill swallowed it. It wasn't quite as hot as earlier in the day, a gentle breeze stirring the air and ruffling Nancy's hair. Down at the pen, most of the bulls had lain down, their jaws moving as they digested their feed.

Two of them were off to one side, their foreheads pressed together, forefeet pawing at the dirt. As we watched, they drew back, then came together with a crash. One stumbled, a leg buckling under his weight. He turned slightly and the other bull seized the advantage, and rammed his head against the other's rib cage, dumping him to the ground. The fallen animal shoved himself up on his forelegs, looked all around dazedly, then got up and trotted away. The victor seemed to be satisfied with that, and made no attempt to follow. Pawing at the ground, he blew through his nostrils, sending the challenge out to the others. After a moment, he lowered his body to the ground and started contentedly chewing his cud.

Nancy turned and faced me. Placing her hands on my arms, she looked up at my face.

"Will the boys find them?" she asked. "Do you have White Wolf and Sun Bird hidden well enough that they'll be fairly safe?"

"The cave is very hard to find," I told her. "You really have to know it's there, or you can't find it. Besides, the range of hills it's in is beyond the J-C fences, so the men shouldn't come anywhere near it. I'm sure they'll be safe."

"I wish it were all over," she said. "I wish they were in that wagon right now, with the Kansas line behind them. You better be thinking up some excuse to go in to Dodge, and haul it out here to the ranch. While you're at it, think of what you'll tell dad, when the wagon's gone."

She turned away, and her hands went up to her face. "I'm at a loss. This seemed so easy, when I first thought it up. Now I realize how hard it will be to explain. You buying it for travel later on, that he'd accept, but what happens when it disappears? When, suddenly, there's no more wagon?"

I put my hand on her shoulder, and turned her toward me. "What happened to the optimistic lady who came up with this plan to begin with? The one who's always looking on the sunny side. Don't worry, Nancy. We aren't going to let anyone around here know about that wagon. We'll sneak it by, somehow, and take it on over to the cave. Might be better if we told Bob Wright not to say anything to your dad, but I can't think of any logical excuse, can you?"

She looked up, and giggled.... "No, but give me time. We could tell him we're running away to be married, and I don't want dad to know." She laughed, and spun on her toes.

I wanted to laugh, but it stuck in my throat. I'd almost decided that tonight was time to tell her about Joe Warner's checkered past, and the possible connection with Specter. I mustn't right now. She was so happy, and planning a future, obviously one in which I'd share. I didn't have the heart.

Sensing something wrong, she stopped twirling and reached for my hand. The twilight was darkening, and she came in close to peer in my face....

"What's the matter, Case? Did I say the wrong thing? Am I assuming too much, when I speak of marriage, and you and I running away to tie the knot? We spoke of love, and where I come from, that means marriage and children. You're not trying to back out, are you?" She shook a mocking finger under my nose, and then reached up and kissed the tip.

I jerked away in consternation, looking all around. The boys had gone into the bunkhouse, and I didn't think Bud and Judah could see from the porch.

"What's wrong? Don't you liked to be kissed? C'mon! Dad probably knows what we're doing down here, anyway." She had a tight grip on my shirt sleeves, her head thrown back, eyes sparkling in the fading light....

Bending, I took her in my arms and kissed her.

Tenderly, at first, but as her soft warmness pressed close, I strained her to me, and my lips grew more demanding....

"Please...No, Case...Case! Leggo, Case!" She pushed her hands, desperately, against my chest, until finally the roaring in my ears quieted, and I released her. She staggered, and put a hand to her mouth. A trickle of blood appeared at one corner. She looked at me in wonder....

Awkwardly, I reached out toward her, feeling helpless as tears appeared on her cheeks. "I'm so sorry, honey! I sure didn't mean to hurt you! Don't know what came over me. You were standing there, a bit of light making your eyes sparkle like diamonds, and your sweet lips just begging to be kissed. Once I got started, I couldn't stop! Aw, hell! Please stop crying! I can't find the right words, but I'm sorry...."

"Yes, Case. I understand, and you weren't to blame. You didn't hurt me that much. It's just that I wasn't prepared. Let's walk a bit, and you tell me more." She took my hand.

"Well, Nancy. As your dad would say, we got us a tanglement. We love each other, and I want you to be my wife, but right now I have nothing to offer. Wait, now! Let me finish what I was gonna say!

"I don't even know for sure who I am. I'm dead broke, a ranch hand for your dad, and with no prospects for a future. I'm not exactly what they call a 'good catch,' at this time. Granted, I was wearing a decent suit of clothes, and had the appearance of a gentleman, so it's possible I have a fortune hidden away somewhere, but I don't have it now.

"Your dad would have to be crazy, to let his only daughter marry a nonperson, with no means to support her. We can joke about running away, and getting married, but I wouldn't ask you to share a hand's cabin, on someone else's ranch. I love you too much for that."

She stopped, and studied me closely.... "You said, 'don't know for sure,' when you spoke of your identity. Could that mean, you have some idea, of who you might be?"

Huh! That had been a slip! Not much got by this bright, quick-witted young lady! What're you gonna do now, Joe?

Motioning her to the fence, I boosted her up and climbed up beside her. Rolling myself a smoke, I told her about the conversation with Sam Wyeth, and the flashbacks I'd experienced after riding the chestnut gelding. Word for word, I repeated exactly what Wyeth had told me, not offering a single excuse for my actions in that saloon. I even told her about the reward, and how the Army'd been determined to hang me.

"But you shot in self-defense!" she cried. "You had men there who could testify to that. Why did you run?"

"That I can't tell you for sure," I replied. "But, this happened in Texas, and even as late as seventy-four, there were those who still fought the War. The troops were still looked upon as Reconstruction forces, and Texans were considered Rebels. Add to that the fact that the men I shot were black, and we now have an 'incident,' not a plain old gunfight."

"Why haven't they arrested you before now? Surely someone would have recognized you, somewhere. Could it be Wyeth is mistaken? That you just resemble this man, Joe Warner?"

"You're forgetting those scenes I described. Maw giving me fits for graining my horse too heavily. Then the one in the kitchen, and my paw telling me goodbye. No! I'm Warner, all right, or I was..." At this point, I stopped. Should I tell her of my fears...of

Frank Specter, and all that he'd mean to our relationship? No! After all, I had nothing but conjecture to go on. The *Harper's* article *could* be purely coincidence. I decided to wait until more memories were brought to mind and I knew for certain I *was* Frank Specter.

Nancy turned, and drew my face down to her's, touching my lips lightly with her own. "What happened in the past has no bearing on our feelings for each other now," she said.

"Whatever you did ten years ago, you're a fine, honorable man, Joe Warner. Your feelings of compassion for the Indians are the best proof of that. No cold-blooded killer would go out of his way to get them free of the fix that they are in now. You had the chance, and certainly the right, to shoot, but you didn't. Instead, here you are, risking your chances to stay on this ranch. Scheming with me to help them get to Montana.... Are you ever going to light that cigarette?"

Reaching into a pocket, she brought out a match, scratching it alight on the top rail. "Here," she said. "You can't very well smoke that cigarette, without fire." She lit it, laughed, and blew out the match. I'd forgotten the smoke I'd rolled.

We sat there for a time, just enjoying each other, and I felt wonderfully complete with her by my side. A nighthawk called, off in the distance, and behind us I could hear contented sounds of bulls settling down for the night. Somehow the worries of my forgotten past were no longer important to me, and I dreamed of a future, with this wonderful girl sharing every moment.

"Case!" She was holding my hand, and shook it gently.

"Yes," I replied. Then... "Unless it's something

I must hear now, I'd just as soon wait. I'm right in the middle of a beautiful dream, and I want to see how it comes out."

"Silly!" she giggled. "We'll have all kinds of time for that sort of thing. Right now, we have to figure out how to get in to Dodge, and pick up the wagon. They'll need food, a rifle, and some tools. More clothing, most of which I have, from old clothes of mine and dad's. Serviceable enough, but we no longer wear them."

"Can you buy those things from Wright, without him wondering what you intend to use them for? We just picked up more grub than a dozen men could eat in a month."

"Sure," she replied. "I'll just tell him the stuff's going out to the line camps. It's a little early, but we'd be buying it soon, anyway. It'll make the rifle and tools easy to explain too. Now, here's what I figure...

"Tomorrow, everybody'll be either gone, or busy branding. I'll sneak out two of the mules, and let down some rails, so the others can get out. It'll look like they knocked down a part of the fence. I've ridden most of those mules, at some time or other, and I'll ride one of 'em now.

"Don't you worry about me being able to drive that wagon. I've handled four-up, since I was twelve years old. Problem now is where to hide the wagon and mules, until we can take it to White Wolf and Sun Bird. Has to be close enough so's I can get back here on foot."

"That's easy," I told her. "We won't hide it. We'll run it on out to the cave the same day. Look! Tomorrow, I'll be the only one on a horse. We'll allow plenty of time for you to do your chore, then I'll accidentally 'discover' that the mules are out. Since

I'll have my brand new cutting horse under me, I'll volunteer to chase 'em down.

"Judah and Bud'll want to get that branding down, and old Buck'll be there to cut 'em in and out. I'll take care and mess up the tracks, so's they can't tell how many I'm after, and I'll meet you somewhere nearby. How's that sound?"

"Fine!" She was grinning in delight, and squeezed my arm affectionately. "That's worth another kiss, my bucko." She leaned over, clasped the back of my head, and kissed me hard on the lips.

"There's a shallow draw, about a mile or so beyond that grove, where mother's buried. I'll meet you there. You can point me in the right direction, and I'll stick with the wagon, while you bring those mules behind. They'll mess up all the wagon tracks, and nobody will suspect. Boy! We're sure smart, you and I! We make a good team!"

"You bet," I laughed. "Is that worth another ki—"

The muffled "boom" of a six-gun shattered the night! Over in the bunkhouse, men were shouting, and a figure darted out of the door, running for the horse corral.

Leaping down off the fence, I ran to head him off. I saw the glint of metal as he raised his arm and pointed at me. The gun roared, the flash blinding me, and I felt a tug near my waistband. Another flash, but I was diving, headlong, my arms wrapping around his legs as I brought him down, and we crashed to the ground. The fall broke my hold.

Cursing, he slashed at me with the gun, landing a blow on my left shoulder that numbed the whole arm. Rolling myself away, legs kicking at the ground, I managed to get an arm around his neck and put on the pressure. I could feel those neck muscles straining as he gasped for air. Suddenly the struggles ceased and he went limp. Cautious, I reached for the gun with my tingling left hand before I released my arm from his neck. He lay motionless in the dirt of the corral, his face upturned to the sky. It was Sim!

Bud helped me to my feet, and Nancy ran into my arms. On the ground, Sim was stirring, his back arching and his arms and legs twitching in spasm. After a moment, he sat up and looked at us, his face twisted in a grimace.

"He cheated me," he gritted out. "I hope he's dead! The skunk held out a card. He got what he deserved."

I whirled toward Bud. His face was black with anger. A lump of muscle bulged at the hinge of his jaw, and his fists were clenched at his sides.

"Who's he talking about?" I cried. "Who got shot?"

"It's Buck," he told me. "Gutshot by this coyote, and at point-blank range. He didn't even have a gun."

"Here!" I handed Sim's gun to Bud. Clemens had the killer in an armlock and was leading him back to the bunkhouse.

Dodging them, I ran to the bunkhouse, Nancy right behind. Laidley, a tow-headed youngster, was standing beside Judah's blocky figure, both gazing down at Buck's body on the floor.

He lay there on his back, his face purpled, and a spreading bloodstain above his belt. Then, as we watched unbelievingly, he groaned and sat up, clutching his middle with both hands. He looked up at us....

"Well, don't jest stand there! Give me a hand up. Whew! Boy! That sure did knock the stuffin' out of me!

"Thanks, fellers. Hang on to me for a minute, will yuh? I still feel sorta woozy. Head feels like it's gonna bust!"

"Lay down on that bunk. The one right over here. I know it's not yours. Whoever belongs to it won't care none. I want to take a look under your shirt."

It was Nancy taking charge, as usual. Ignoring his wails of protest, we stretched him out on the bed and I unbuttoned the shirt. Carefully I loosened his belt and showed them the badly dented buckle. A thick, solid brass rectangle, it featured a spread eagle and thirteen stars, and was normally worn by cavalrymen. Lead splashes streaked the crevices.

On his abdomen, we found several deep lacerations bleeding freely, but none serious. Nancy set about cleaning them up, and ordered me to bring boiling water from the kitchen.

Buck was a lucky fellow and, judging from the black looks on the faces of my friends, so was Sim. If Buck had died, I was certain he would have been decorating the nearest tree. Many times justice was swift and sure on the frontiers. A man caught in the act, with his guilt a foregone conclusion, wasted no judge's and jury's time with useless arguments. He was often tried and executed on the spot.

I hurried back with the hot water. Buck was half reclined on the bed, his back braced with a saddle and several of our blankets. In his hand was a glass of whiskey, and Fong, the Chinese cook, stood by with a bottle. Buck gestured with the glass....

"Here's to yuh, boys. You've saved my life, and that's a mighty white thing for yuh to do. Here I was bleedin' plumb to death, and y'all come in here, picked me off the floor, a pore, bleedin' wreck of a man, and patched me up. An' you...Miss Nancy, yore wunnerful...Ain't she, boys...Wunnerful, tha's wha' you are, Missy...Mebbe I'll go sleep...now..."

He'd drained the glass, and from the looks of the bottle, he'd drunk half a quart. Lying there, head lolling, he'd begun to snore, sonorously. We took away the saddle and blankets, and covered him up.

"He'll have him a sore belly for a few days, but he'll be all right," Judah told us. "What should we do with this two-bit badman? Far as I'm concerned, we can string him up now. Ain't his fault that Buck's not dead, or dyin'. He meant to kill him, and over a penny-ante poker game, of all things."

Sim was slumped in a chair, his wrists tied securely with latigo thongs. He was scared, there was no doubt about that, but he was still defiant.

"Buck was cheatin' me. I suspicioned he was holding out, but I couldn't ketch him, 'til that last hand. I knowed it, and that's why I shot him. I ain't a damn bit sorry for it."

Judah leaned over him, his face only inches away. In his measured voice he asked a question....

"How much was in the pot? The last one, I mean. The one you almost killed a man over?"

"Well." Sim thought for a moment. "Ante was a nickel, so that's twenty cents. First bet was a dime, and we all called. That put it to sixty cents. I opened for a quarter, and Clemens called. Buck raised a quarter, so now the pot's at a dollar sixty. Laidley folded his cards, I called the raise, and Clemens dropped out."

He wet his lips, puckered his brow, and stared up at the ceiling. Then he smiled, triumphantly! "Why that there pot had a dollar eighty-five cents in it!" he cried.

Judah turned away in disgust. "Pack his outfit, and get him ready to leave. I'll go fetch what he has coming to him. He don't own no horse of his own, so throw his saddle on one of them scrubs we picked up last gather."

Halfway out the door, he turned. "Give him his gun, but I don't want him to have a single cartridge. Look through his saddle bags, and all his gear. Make sure he's clean."

I went out to the horse corral and Nancy tagged along, a lantern in her hand. There were three of the runty scrubs I had to choose from, and I picked the worst of the lot. Took only a minute to drop a rope over his head and lead him out of the corral, where I slapped on Sim's saddle and bridle.

Laidley and Clemens brought the would-be killer out a few minutes later, and he climbed onto the horse. He sat there by the fence and looked down on us, his manner truculent. The fright was all gone, now that he knew we'd permit him to go, and his bravado was back in full force.

"You two," he pointed toward Laidley and Clemens. "I'll ketch you in town, one of these times. Make you wish that I *had* been hung!" He glanced toward Nancy, but he must surely have known that one wrong word about her would bring the rest of us down on him like a ton of hard rock, and he held his tongue.

I came last, and he took his time with me. He looked all up and down my frame, then said his piece.

"Mister! You, I'm gonna take special care of, soon. You and your high and mighty way, and your fancy manners. Don't even know your proper name, and they let you sleep in one of their bedrooms. Treat you like one of the family. Hadn't been for you, I'd have got out of here, first try, and not had to take a lot of lip from that old man in there. So, I owe you somethin' special. Ain't nothin' gonna happen right away. I want you to sweat some. Keep on lookin' over your shoulder, and one of these days, there I'll be. That's a promise, buster!"

I looked up at him, and grinned. "I'll go you one better, *buster*. If I ever *see* you again, anywhere, I'll figure that you're there to collect, and I'll shoot you where you stand. That's my promise, buster!"

With a curse, he yanked the scrub's head around and sank his spurs. A moment later, he was out of sight.

CHAPTER TWELVE

TUESDAY MORNING DAWNED at five o'clock, and showed promise of the fine weather expected in late June. I'd gotten up more'n an hour before that, and Nancy had fixed us a big breakfast we shared in the ranch kitchen. Naturally there had been a lot of handholding, and a stolen kiss or two, and breakfast was longer than usual. Old Charley Fong had watched with amusement, and added a comment from time to time in his quaint, pidgin English.

I was walking about two feet off the ground when I passed the bunkhouse. Clemens was standing by the door, a towel around his neck and lather on his face. He waved me in....

"C'mere, Case! You gotta see this. It's somethin' else. Hurry up, 'fore he hides!"

I ran up three steps, and went inside. Buck stood by his bunk, his back to me, and his head down.

"G'wan Buck," Clemens called. "Turn around, and show him yore belly!" He was laughing, and so was Laidley.

Buck finally turned, sheepishly. He really looked awful! The aftereffects of drinking all that whiskey had left him haggard, and he looked like an old man.

His bloodshot eyes, surrounded by dark rings, stared at me owlishly, and he had some difficulty keeping his balance.

He was wearing the bottom half of his longjohns, and his boots, and he'd unwound the bandage Nancy had applied on the night before. A massive bruise covering his entire midriff showed above his waistband. The deep livid purple testified to the force of the blow delivered by the heavy-caliber bullet.

"It's a dumb thing to ask," I told him. "But how does it feel? I imagine it's pretty sore, huh? Maybe you ought not to be on your feet. Perhaps it'd be better to baby that for a while. No telling how much damage it did inside."

He grinned, ruefully. "Thanks, but no thanks. If I stay in bed for long, I will be sick. Best thing's to keep goin'. That way I won't stiffen up. It ain't my belly that's botherin' me, so much as this head. Boy! I must have drunk the bottle dry! Mouth tastes like somebody'd left their boots'n dirty socks in there. Phui!"

"Tell you what," I told him. "You go on out, and put your whole head in the horse tank. Leave it under, as long's you can. Come up, grab a breath, and then go under again. Keep on doing that, until I get back. I'm gonna bring you back a cure for what ails you. Go on, now. Go duck your head!"

As he started out the door, I hollered at him to put on a pair of pants. "And take a towel along, too!" I added.

In the ranch kitchen, I explained to Fong what I required for Buck's hangover, and he brought them to me. At first, I had trouble explaining Buck's ailment. Then, with gestures, I demonstrated swigging down the whiskey, and repeated that several times. Lastly, I pantomimed bleary eyes and an aching head. Finally he nodded, a big smile on his face.

"Oh! He dlunk! Moh bettah, he dlink lotta watah, and he walk belly slow. Plitty soon, he moh bettah, you bet!"

Into a pint mason jar of cold water, I dissolved a tablespoon of baking soda. Then I added some cinnamon and a few drops of lemon extract and stirred the mixture. Grabbing a pot of coffee, I went back to the bunkhouse.

If Buck didn't feel any better, at least he had improved appearancewise. His hair was combed, and he was a lot more steady on his feet. I stirred the mixture again and handed it to him.

"Drink that right down, Buck. Don't stop 'til that's bone dry! Go on, now. It won't hurt you."

Like a lamb going to the slaughter, he tipped up the jar and drank it all down. With a wry grimace, he handed me the jar, and I swapped him a cup of black coffee.

With Sim gone and Buck in bad shape, the plans Nancy and I had made for today might have to be changed. My best bet would be to wait until Judah finished breakfast. He'd tell us who would do what, and where. Though I'd already eaten, I decided to sit down with the rest and at least drink some coffee.

Buck had finished his first cup, and was pouring another. The sick look was gone, and he was obviously feeling better. As I watched, he propped up a boot and started buckling his spurs, so apparently he figured on working today. That made me feel much more optimistic about our plans.

"I'm gonna go grain my horse," I told him. "I'll see you at breakfast. Might be a good idea to ask old Fong for some hot chiles, and chop 'em up with your eggs. If you can take the heat, they'll do a lot toward settling your stomach."

He nodded, and I went on out of the bunkhouse.

Judah and Bud were just going through the kitchen door so I'd have to hustle, if I wanted to hear what he had to say.

The gelding's head was up, and he stretched his neck and whickered as I came through the barn. I led him outside to the tank and let him drink a bit of water, then back in the stall for a short ration of oats and some hay.

"Today's a big day for you," I told him. "Your first day on the job, so you'd better be on your best behavior. Don't mind a little jumping around, first off, but once we start a bull into that chute, I want your full attention...."

If he heard me, he sure didn't acknowledge it. Just kept chomping away on the grain, and snorting when the chaff got up his nose. I went out of the barn laughing....

Mister, I said to myself, everything's sure enough going your way, about now. You got the old world by the tail on a downhill pull. Good friends, a boss who likes you, and the sweetest girl in the world wanting to be your wife! You're a lucky man, Joe Warner! A lucky man!

As I started up the steps to the kitchen door, I realized a buckboard was coming up the ranch road with a horsebacker following behind. From the light mane and tail, it looked a whole lot like Tilghman's blood bay. I waited, with my hand on the railing....

As they came closer, I could see it was Bill, but the men in the buckboard were strangers. Hearing the noise, Bud got up from the table and peered through the screen door.

"Who is it, Case?" he asked. "Mighty early for company."

I told him it was Tilghman with a couple of strangers in a rig, and he came on out, Judah following close behind. The rest of the boys were crowding the doorway, and Nancy was in behind, straining to get a look at our visitors.

Tilghman got down and tied his horse. He nodded to all as he removed his gloves. One of the two men in the rig was vaguely familiar to me, but I couldn't place him.

"Mornin', everybody," Bill said. "Miss Nancy." He touched his hat brim. "I want you all to meet a couple fellers."

It was Judah who spoke first. "You're just in time," he said. "We're jest sittin' down to breakfast. We got more'n enough to go around. Let's go inside, and you can make your introductions there."

Once everyone was seated, Tilghman indicated the chunkier of the two men, who wore a full beard. "That there feller's Mr. William A. Pinkerton. You mebbe heard of his paw. He's the one worked for Mr. Lincoln, during the War. Well. They have the Pinkerton Agency now, with branches in Chicago, and New York. William, here, runs the Chicago office."

The other man, clean-shaven, and in his mid-thirties, was looking my way, and seemed apprehensive for some reason. I smiled at him, but he hurriedly looked away....

Bill continued. "This other feller is a salesman. His name's Lyle Newcomb, and he works for a well-known outfit in Chicago, also. Hibbard, Spencer and Bartlett! Does that ring a bell with you, Case?"

I looked at him in surprise. That was the company my new friend Zimmerman had suggested I contact. What was he doing here? What did he want from me?

Judah spoke up. "We're very happy to meet you gentlemen, but this food'll git cold, if we don't eat it right now. We can hear what this is all about, after breakfast!"

Newcomb's face was flushed, and he looked uncomfortable. He shoved back his chair and stood up, obviously embarrassed at having interrupted a meal, but determined to speak his piece.

"You men go right ahead and eat your breakfast. What I'm about to say concerns only this man." He pointed to me. "I have been told," he continued, "that because of your injury, you have been unable to remember your own name, or even your past life. I am here to help you. I..." he faltered, holding on to the chair back for support.

He stared at me, his face a mask of fright! For a moment, he was unable to continue. Then he straightened up, and for a second or two he looked up at the ceiling.

"It was an accident," he said. "You must believe me! We had both been drinking. I, perhaps, more than you, and I do confess that I was somewhat aggravated by the fact that your attitude was complete indifference. You refused to accept a single statement that I had made." He looked at me again.

"You don't have the slightest idea about what I am telling you, do you?" he said. "Well, from the beginning...

"We boarded the same train at Kansas City. You planned a visit to Santa Fe, and I was going through to Albuquerque. I overheard part of your conversation with another fellow, on the station platform, and I recognized your name immediately. I want to tell you, I was impressed! To think that I'd be sharing a car, perhaps even a seat, with Frank Specter!"

I jumped to my feet! "Are you saying that I'm Specter? That can't be! I can't be Frank Specter! You're lying! Who put you up to this? What's your game?"

Tilghman and Bud had me by the arms, and they held me. "Take it easy, Case," said Bud. "Let the man have a moment to say his piece. We want to hear him, and so should you!" I sat back down in the chair, heart pounding.

"That's right, Mr. Specter. You *are* Frank Specter! Known all over the west as one of the fastest men in America. My business is guns! Colt handguns! And for me to meet you in the flesh was one of the greatest things ever happened to me.

"We did share a seat, and we had breakfast together. The conductor sold me a bottle of brandy, and we had a libation or two during the course of the morning. I showed you that sample case of mine, and you admired the weapons in it. The one you seemed most interested in was the long-barreled thirty-eight Police Model. I told you we called it a Cop and Thug.

"Later in the morning, I'm afraid you became bored with my company. I'll admit that I was somewhat carried away, in an attempt to make you commit yourself to specific likes, as to manufacturer and models. You might even say that I was insistent! I don't believe you were angry, just tired of petty conversation.

"You excused yourself, and went out onto the platform, at the end of the car. After a few minutes, I had another pull on the bottle, and followed you outside. Excusing myself, I took a stand on the other side, and pleaded a need for a bit of fresh air.

"I'd carried the bottle out in my coat pocket, and, using the coat as cover, I sneaked another drink. My courage bolstered somewhat, I pointed out potential targets, suggesting you try your skill with one of my sample guns. When you refused, I'm afraid I threw caution aside, and literally dared you to try. Intimated that the stories I'd heard were all exaggerated falsehoods.

"Even then, you refused to be angered. Somewhat amusedly, you told me that I was entitled to think what I wanted, and said you were going inside. When you placed your hand on my shoulder, to move me out of your way, I panicked! I thought you planned to strike me! With the case still in my hand, I swung at you, with all of my might. To my horror, the force of the blow caused you to lose your balance, and you toppled from the platform.... Wait, please! Let me finish telling my story. I'll be glad to answer your questions.

"The train was moving very fast, and I was afraid you had fallen beneath the wheels. You would have been killed! The emergency cord was just inside the door, but I was paralyzed with fear! It had been an accident! But it wouldn't make a bit of difference to a jury. I'd still be guilty of murder! I knew that pulling the cord couldn't bring you back, when the wheels had literally chopped you in half. Nothing could undo the harm that I had caused, in my drunkenness, so I decided to say nothing. It wasn't until I had gotten back into my seat that I realized the case was gone. It had been ripped out of my hand by the blow."

He held up his hand as I started to speak.... "I'm about to the end of my narrative. I beg your indulgence, please.

"When the train reached Santa Fe, I claimed your luggage as part of my own, and of course I carried your coat off, on my arm. I found later that it contained your wallet, which held your identification, and of course, your money. No one seemed to have missed you, even the conductor, but I knew it couldn't remain a secret for long. Your employer would miss you, of course, and any investigation would lead straight to me.

"I decided to give myself up, and immediately wired Pinkerton's, telling them briefly what had occurred. Since that train had been only a few miles from Dodge City at the time of the accident, Mr. Pinkerton suggested that we meet here, and determine if the body had been found.

"We both arrived last evening, and contacted your Marshal Tilghman. To my happy surprise, he told us you had survived that terrible accident. I am so sorry, Mr. Specter! I hope you can find it in your heart to forgive me. Anything I can do to make things right for you, please don't hesitate. My resources are limited, but whatever recompense you deem proper, I will endeavor to provide. Again . . . I'm very sorry!"

Well, after all that, I really didn't know what to say, I was angry, of course, but nothing was to be gained by making this man any sorrier than he'd already demonstrated. Right now the best thing for me to do was to gather up my things, and leave the Clayton ranch. I knew they'd want no more to do with me, now that my real identity was known.

I couldn't bring myself to shake his hand, but I did say that I understood how he had felt, and didn't hold any hard feelings for him.

"Took guts for you to come here, and tell what happened on the train," I told him. "You sure didn't plan for it to happen, so it really was an accident. I thank you for coming forward with the truth. Hadn't been for you, I'd still be wondering who, and what, I am. Did you bring my things, by any chance? My luggage, and my coat?"

"Yes. Of course," he replied. "They're out in the buckboard. Everything's there, including the two derringers in the special pockets."

I glanced at him. "What special pockets?" I asked.

"I forgot," he apologized. "I guess it may take a

while for you to remember all of the things in your past. I will be glad to show you. Very clever, actually."

Nancy's face was a study, and I could imagine what might be running through her mind. She had understood Joe Warner, and could sympathize with him. After all, his gunfight came looking for him. But Specter was a different breed of cat.

Or was he? Here I was condemning myself, when in reality I knew very little about Frank Specter. Actually, the story in *Harper's* had been the first, and the last, I'd ever heard of him. Maybe I wasn't giving myself a fair shake.

Once outside, Newcomb motioned to me, and I joined him at the rear of the buckboard. He opened a large carton, taking out a brown suit coat. A match for the trousers I'd worn on first coming to the ranch. It was freshly brushed.

"Look here," he said. He held the end of one sleeve open, then reached up into the armpit and pulled on something. A cloth-covered metal panel slid back, exposing a small, flat handgun with a spur trigger. Releasing whatever he'd pulled allowed the panel to spring back in place, concealing it again. It seemed to be constructed very professionally.

"It's a Frank Wesson superposed pistol," he said. "There is another in the other sleeve. As you can see, they have a pair of barrels that pivot on a base pin. Both are chambered for the forty-one rimfire cartridge. Not effective at a range much over twenty feet, but it will do the job. They are single action, and must be cocked each time. After firing, you press this catch in front of the trigger, and twist the barrels a half turn. That brings another load up ready to fire, so you have four shots, using both guns. Perhaps you'd care to try them, Mr. Specter? Who knows, it might help you somehow, in recovering your memory. You know, familiar things...It might be worth the effort."

"Sure!" I told him. "Why not?" He helped me as I shrugged into the coat and adjusted the lapels.

"A very soft, braided cord leads up each sleeve." He let me see the cord, an endless leather strip, which led over my shoulders and down the other sleeve.

"Merely by bunching your shoulders, you apply enough tension to open the pockets, allowing both weapons to drop into your hands."

The coat fit perfectly. I looked around the yard, seeing that a wind gust had blown the paper carton out of the buckboard, and left it on the ground about fifteen feet away.

"You mean like this," I told him. I brought my hands up, the fabric tightening across my shoulders, and felt the guns fall into my hands, where I cocked and fired them both in a smooth, continuous motion. It sounded like a single report, and took place in a fraction of a second.

Newcomb ran out, and brought back the carton. He pointed at the two holes. They overlapped. He was enthusiastic! I shrugged out of the coat and smiled tolerantly.

"Once I got the coat on," I told him, "I knew what to do. It was like a reflex. Apparently, I must have practiced the draw many times, until it became an instinctive movement."

All the boys were crowded around the buckboard, trying to get a look at the carton. Bud was shaking his head in awe, and even Judah had a smile on his face. Tilghman pushed his way through the bunch, and held out his hand.

"I'm pleased to remake your acquaintance," he

said. "We got off on the right foot, you and I, and I'd like it to remain that way. Forget that remark I made about 'hired gun.' In a sense, I'm no different than you. Still friends?"

"Why sure, Bill," I told him. "Surest thing you know. I value your friendship, and I wasn't certain you'd take kindly to me being Frank Specter." I was looking over the heads of the crowd, and didn't see Nancy anywhere.

"Where'd Nancy go?" I asked him. "Did you see her leave? I'd swear she was just behind, when we came out here."

"I don't know," he replied. "Like you said, she came out with the rest of us. Mebbe she's gone to help Fong clean up the kitchen."

"Uh huh... Well, I'd best go hunt her up, and see if she still thinks I'm one of the good guys. Hold off going back to Dodge, will you? I have more to discuss with Newcomb."

Nancy wasn't in the kitchen, and Fong hadn't noticed anything untoward in her actions.

"Mebbeso, she flaid of you, missah Spectah. I look outee window. Heah gun go boom boom. I flaid then. I flaid guns, I no flaid you, missa Spectah. You good man, you betchee."

I ran up the stairs to the second floor. The door to her room was ajar, but the room itself was empty. Then, suddenly, I knew where she would be. The grove out in back, where her mother lay buried...

She was leaning against a tree, her head down, and turned away from me. She gave a start when she heard me coming, a visible shudder that almost made my heart stop beating.

"Please," she whispered. "Don't come any closer. I must have time to think. It has all happened so suddenly, and we both need time to adjust."

"I know," I told her. "But, no matter what my name might be, I'm still the man you professed to love. The past isn't real, even to me, Nancy. Now! That's what counts! How can your feelings change, because of something I did so long ago? Things that even I still don't remember clearly."

She turned and faced me, her eyes red from crying.... "I still love you, Case. That will never change! It's whether or not I want to be married to a man whose life is literally on the line, every day he goes to work. That's what I've got to decide, now." She held up her hand. "No, wait....Let me have my say, please!

"I've talked to Flora Tilghman, many times. I've even asked her how she can sleep, while Bill is out there, fair game for any would-be badman who comes along? She *can't* sleep, at least not soundly. It's as simple as that. She worries all the time, and would give anything if Bill would turn in his badge and raise cattle, or do anything, so long as he would quit carrying a gun for a living."

"I couldn't promise you that," I told her. "I haven't my memory back, as yet. Bits and pieces, yes, but not totally. There may be men in my past who won't let me quit. Men who carried a fancied grievance, or just want to try me, and see who comes out on top. That's a fact of my life, or what was my life, before.

"We can find us a place, somewhere, and raise our cattle, and horses. I'd like to raise horses, especially. But, one day I might turn around, and have to face some man who wanted to be known as the faster gun. I can't deny that, Nancy. But can't we give it a try?"

"I can't say anything right now, Case. I need more time. Be patient with me, please. Don't leave the ranch. Keep on working for Dad, just as you have been, and give me time for thought. I'll try to work things out. Now, go! Please!"

She had started to cry again as I turned away. This day had begun so beautifully.... I headed back toward the buckboard, and Lyle Newcomb.

CHAPTER
THIRTEEN

THAT NIGHT I went to bed with a lot on my mind. In the suitcase returned by Newcomb, I'd found my personal papers, and learned I had accounts in several banks. It added up to a sizeable amount. More than enough to buy and fully stock a fine ranch. A copy of my contract with Pinkerton was there also, and showed the date and place of my birth—1849, in Virginia. I was thirty-five, then; older than I had estimated from my appearance, and Nancy's senior by fourteen years. I wondered if that would matter to her.

There were three Colt revolvers in the case. Two were in a double holster rig. Blued .44-40s, with the shorter barrels and one-piece walnut grips. The other gun was a beautifully engraved .45, silver-plated, with the long barrel. I found an inscription engraved on the backstrap: "*In grateful appreciation—Frank Specter From Allan Pinkerton July 1883.*"

William Pinkerton had told me that his father was critically ill, and wasn't expected to live. I wondered what coup I'd accomplished to earn such a prize? Then I decided that I'd just as soon not know....

In addition to my suitcase, there was a large canvas bag, in which I found a rather plain saddle of excellent quality and workmanship, as well as a split-eared headstall, with an unusual silver-mounted bit. Both the saddle and the double-holster rig were made by a Frank Meanea in Cheyenne.

As I lay there, I went over the events of the day. Judah and the rest hadn't seemed bothered by my new identity. The only one who had balked was Nancy. Well, about all that remained would be for someone to decide he wanted a piece out of me. A gunfight now would be the proverbial last straw. We'd never get married!

Eventually, I did go to sleep, but all night I rolled and tossed as a steady procession of gun-belted men hollered for me to come out in the street and prove that I was a man!

The rest of that week went fast, and next thing I knew, I was getting ready to go to Dodge City. Nancy had been avoiding me religiously, and we hadn't spoken since that day I'd learned my true identity. The boys and I had branded all of the bulls and taken them to the high pasture, where Clemens had already found and destroyed the stray piebald bull. My pal Buck was doing fine, and seemed not to be bothered with his assortment of bruises. He and Laidley had taken over as fence riders, while Bud, Judah, and I spent our time with the cattle. Fall was coming soon, and Judah was figuring on marketing all of his three- and four-year-old steers. It had been a mild summer, and even though the year before hadn't had a normal rainfall, the graze was lush. All of the cattle were fat, and some of his steers would weigh over twelve hundred. We'd drifted most of them into pastures, separate from those being grazed by the cow-calf pairs, and the fall roundup was expected to go smoothly.

I'd named my new horse Amigo, because he'd turned out to be a perfect partner, and we'd done our share in those four days. What I'd learned, apparently as a boy in Texas, came back to me, albeit slowly. Amigo anticipated most of what I planned, and sometimes went me one better by making his own decisions.

Only yesterday, he'd saved me from what would have been, at best, a bad mauling. I'd been daydreaming about Nancy when he changed directions suddenly, in dodging after a mulish range bull. I landed on my back with the breath all knocked out of me. That bull'd decided I was the enemy, so he tucked in his chin and charged me, that hornless head only inches off the ground. Amigo had stopped when my weight left his back, and he bounded at the bull, smashing into his shoulder and hurling him to the ground. Then he spun around and let drive with both of his hind feet into the bull's rear quarter. This time, the bull was only too happy to call it quits.

Poor Clemens had gotten the dirty job, but we all agreed he'd really asked for it. Bud'd mentioned that he had some "clean" work that had to be done. Clemens, who only moments before had been joshing Buck and his new partner about patching up line camps, volunteered. Right now he was trying to restore some semblance of shine to his boots for the festivities in Dodge. He wasn't having much success.

Bud had put him to cleaning out the numerous springs and clogged water holes on the ranch. Which meant he'd stood in knee-deep mud and water most of the time, and what had been done to the boots was barely equaled by the damage suffered by his pride. He blamed Buck for some obscure reason, vowing he wouldn't rest until they were even.

Since Tilghman counted on my help in judging the race, I decided to wear my one suit. There had been a box of shells for the Wesson derringers tucked away in my suitcase, and I naturally included them in my costume. The double rig would have been ostentatious, I figured, especially since the town had undoubtedly been alerted to my identity as Specter. The last thing I wanted to do was to "look the part," so I wore Judah's rig. The one he'd loaned me earlier. I had returned Newcomb's sample, of course, and I was carrying one of my own revolvers. Glancing into the mirror, I decided I'd pass inspection, but I could have used a new hat. Mine had seen better days. I'd have to stop by Wright and Beverly's and look over their selection.

"C'mon, Clemens!" Buck hollered. "Them boots look dandy! We gotta git to gittin', or we'll be late for the race! The dern thing starts at two o'clock. I figger on making a pile of money, bettin' on that feller, Hogan, and I want to git a bet down, before the odds go to hell."

It being only a week to payday, Judah had given all of us a ten-dollar draw. I hoped Buck would have sense enough to hang on to part of it. I supposed Nancy would be going, but she hadn't made an appearance. Bud had brought up the buckboard, and it was parked in front of the house, so I figured she must be planning to go.

Clemens had given up on making the boots shine, and had drawn them on. They did look pretty sad, the tops all curled over and the toes turned up. He stood there rubbing one against the back of his leg, a disgusted look on his face.

"Maybe you'll win some money," I told him. "Then you can buy a brand new pair."

His face brightened. "Yeah!" he said. "Mebbe I

will! I hear the odds are three to one against the black feller. A bet on him, would bring me thirty dollars back. That is, if I bet my whole wad. Reckon I'll do jest that!"

Moments later we were on our way. It was a grand day, a bright sun and a cloudless sky insuring good weather for a race. Amigo fretted at being held down to a lope, but I had no intention of riding in to Dodge on a lathered horse. When we reached the main road, it was crowded with wagon traffic and men on horseback. I saw old Rufus Shelby in that same, mud-caked buckboard, but we were past him before he realized it was me. I heard him call out, but didn't turn around.

"Look's like everybody in the County's plannin' to show," said Laidley. "I hear Masterson and Tilghman're gonna be the judges, and that could be some fun in itself. Them two have had their differences, from time to time."

"Huh!" Clemens snorted. "Yore plumb loco, Laidley. Bill and Bat've been pals since they were younkers, back in them buffalo huntin' days. Bat had to arrest Tilghman twice, but both times he was freed right away. One time, it was a pure case of mistook identity. Feller named Tillman used to hang out with the Dave Rudabaugh gang. He spelled his name somewhat different from Bill. No! Them two're closer'n fleas on a hound dawg. You can lay money on that!"

As we entered Dodge, we split up. I wanted to know where Tilghman planned for me to be during the race. I'd figured to catch him at his office, then I wanted to swing on by the Wright and Beverly store to buy a new hat. Buck, Laidley, and Clemens headed for Hamilton Bell's Varieties. The bartender there, Bat Masterson's brother George, was booking the bets on today's foot race, and they were in a

hurry to make their wagers. All three had decided
to bet on Hogan, since he was the underdog and
would pay the best odds, providing he won.

"We'll see you down by the depot," said Buck.
"That race starts at two o'clock, and they're gonna
run down the tracks."

"Right!" I nodded, and waved them on. "See you
boys later. Don't go trying to drink that bar dry, and
keep a lookout for Sim. He could be hunting for
more trouble, and this time your belt buckle might
not save your bacon."

They laughed derisively, and went on down the
road, bold threats of what they'd do to Sim floating
back to me. Buck wouldn't be caught unawares a
second time, I was certain.

A buckboard tied in front of Tilghman's office
held four cases of various liquors between the seats.
Looked like we might be having quite a party. Inside, Bill was in a heated discussion with two other
men. They broke off as I entered, and Tilghman took
time to introduce me to them.

"This here's Frank Specter, gentlemen. The man
I've been telling you about. Frank's just now finding
out who he was, having been struck on the head last
month, and suffering the loss of his memory."

"Frank, this here is His Honor Mr. George Hoover. Hoover is our newly elected Mayor, here in
Dodge. He's also in the business of sellin' liquor,
both in his store and across the bar, in his saloon."
We shook hands, and Hoover smiled.

"It's a real pleasure, Mr. Specter," he said. "I had
the honor of chatting with Mr. Pinkerton yesterday,
and he certainly speaks highly of you. Welcome to
our fair city."

The other man was watching closely, a faint smile
showing on his slightly rounded face. He was wearing a black bowler hat, seldom seen in the western

states, and a well-tailored black suit. A diamond-studded horseshoe pin sparkled in his cravat, and the ivory butt of a Frontier Colt jutted from an elaborately tooled, cross-draw holster.

"I'm William Masterson." He held out his hand. "My folks were Canadian, and baptized me Bartholomew. That shortened to Bart, but they pronounced it 'Bat'. Somehow, that stuck, and most folks call me Bat, to this day. Anything's better than Bartholomew!" He laughed, and we all joined in.

Tilghman glanced at his watch. "We'd best be leavin'," he told us. "It's goin' on one, and there are some necessary things to be done. Frank, I'm goin' to appoint you a deputy for just this one day. Pays five dollars, and gives you the authority to wear that gun." He reached into a desk drawer and brought out a six-pointed star.

"Repeat after me: I, Frank Specter, promise to uphold the laws of Dodge City, County of Ford, State of Kansas, enforcing those laws to the best of my ability. So help me, God."

I rattled off that oath, and he pinned on the badge. The others seemed to approve, and I was pleased to be given such trust when I was in fact a stranger. Bill asked if I wanted to ride with them in the buckboard. I declined, and explained about stopping at Bob Wright's store.

He glanced up at my hat, which really was in bad shape, a grin on his face....

"Fine! See you at the depot, then. You'd best leave your horse tied at the store. Even standing room will be hard to find, with all those folks watching the race. There will be shade on the east side by the stairs, and water aplenty."

I glanced down at my vest. With my coat unbuttoned, that gold star gleamed in the sunlight. I'd worn a badge in the past, but somehow this situation was far different.

"Please accept my thanks," I told Bill. "From a man who really appreciates what you have done here. With your trust in me, you've restored my faith in myself. I won't abuse my privileges, you can bank on that!"

Declining the offer of one for the road, I went out where Amigo waited, stamping irritably, tied at the hitching post. Jerking loose the reins, I climbed into the saddle, and went on down the street. As I passed the Signal Office, the telegrapher was standing in the doorway. He waved, and I waved back.

"Howdy do, Mr. Specter!" he hollered. "Fine day for racing, isn't it?" He smiled.

Well, I thought to myself. It sure doesn't take long for news to get around. Of course he probably had business with Bill Tilghman every day, and might have inquired after me.

Turning onto Front Street, I looked across at the station platform. It was already crowded, and more folks were headed toward it. Others were taking up positions along the tracks. Small tents had been put up for the contestants, and as I watched, the white man, Sawyer, came out of his and waved to his following. A cheer went up, and advice was volunteered by all.

Approaching Wright and Beverly's, I recognized two familiar faces; those of Sim and the black-bearded man with whom I'd had the early encounter. As I watched, they turned in to the Alamo Saloon, next door to the Long Branch. Their stumbling gait attested to the fact that they had been drinking. The malevolent glare of the bearded man and the truculence displayed by Sim made me guess I was the topic of their drunken discussion.

I rode around on the side of the building, tied Amigo to an iron post provided for that purpose, and loosened the saddle cinches. A water trough was nearby, and I made sure that he could reach it. My carbine I took inside the store, where I handed it to a clerk for safekeeping. Wright was at the rear of the store, and waved at me.

"I'll be through here in a moment," he hollered. "You go ahead and look around a bit." The clerk stowed my Winchester under the counter, and showed me the hat section, then stood by as I tried some on. I found one that I liked for color and design, but it was too small, so he went back into the stockroom to look for one in a larger size.

I wandered over into the boot department and tried a few pairs. One in particular, a pair made by Justin, fit like a glove. Bob Wright picked that moment to come by, and complimented me on my choice of boots.

"Those are about the best in the store. Justin's shop is small, and he only makes a few pair each week. We wish that he'd get a bigger place, and hire some help. I could sell a lot more, if we had 'em."

The clerk brought out a hat that fit me, so I went to the front counter with Wright to settle up. I'd found more than nine hundred in the wallet returned by Newcomb, so I paid my balance on the wagon, as well.

"Thanks, Frank. Do you mind my calling you that? We all heard the good news, and we wish you the best of luck in remembering all of your past. I'm surprised that someone didn't recognize you. You're pretty famous, you know."

"Yeah!" I told him. "Probably just as well they didn't." I handed him my old boots and hat. "Could you wrap these up for me? Never know when an extra hat or boots might come in handy. I'll just put 'em out in the wagon. Bring in a team sometime the first of the week, and get it out of your way."

Wright put them in a carton. "We're gonna close up soon, and go watch the race," he told me. "We'll open again, when the race is over. Perhaps I'll see you there."

I nodded, then remembered about Amigo. He assured me the horse would be fine just where I tied him, so I thanked him and left the store.

Rounding the corner, I found Sim and his bearded friend standing next to the wagon. Amigo was all right, but he was side-stepping nervously and pulling against the tied rein.

"Thought we'd have a little talk, you and I," Sim leered. "Didn't have no idea I was foolin' around with a big, dangerous gunfighter, or I'd've been some careful how I talked."

Blackbeard was nervous, and he showed it. "C'mon Sim. Git it over with. Tell him what we want from him!"

"Oh, yeah." Sim pulled a folded paper from an inside coat pocket, and opened it wide for me to read. It was a reward poster, and the wanted man was Joe Warner. One hundred dollars would be paid for him, dead or alive, by the U.S. Army authorities.

"Imagine," said Sim. "They had this still hanging in the post office across the street. Now, I jest happen to know we got the right man. Joe Warner and Frank Specter are one and the same. I was in Jacksboro when you shot them two troopers. Only thing was, you're older, and I didn't place you.

"Now, me'n my friend here, we don't have no love for that Army neither, so if you'll jest peel out 'bout five hundred dollars off'n that roll yore carryin', we'll be on our way. You won't see us again, and nobody'll be the wiser. You'll be home free."

I shrugged my shoulders in resignation, and

reached in my pocket. Blackbeard, his eyes glittering, snatched at my wallet in his eagerness. I let it fall to the ground, and when he bent down to retrieve it, I slid out my Colt and smashed it against the side of his head. He grunted, then collapsed in a heap.

Swung around to face Sim, I eared the hammer back to full cock, and stared into his frightened face.

"Any reason why I shouldn't put one into your guts, Sim?" I asked. "You've given me more reason than most."

"I ain't wearin' no gun!" he cried. "Besides, I wouldn't stand a chance agin' you, and you know it. It'd be murder!" His expression changed to one of cunning, and he pointed his finger at the Colt.

"I'll fight yuh," he told me. "You take off that gunbelt, and we'll go at it bare knuckle, or are you afeered to fight with yore hands." He sneered.... 'That's the way *men* settle their differences." His fists were down at his sides, opening and closing in anticipation as he waited for my answer.

I studied him in silence. The colossal nerve and uncaring gall of the man rubbed me raw, and I wanted to pound him into the ground. He was shorter than I, but outweighed me a good forty pounds. I'd seen demonstrations of his strength, and knew him to be the stronger man. But I had to show him that two could play at the game of hurting others. Whipping him to a bloody finish was the only language he'd understand.

I motioned him away from the wagon with the barrel of my Colt, then unbuckled the belt, holstered the gun, and stowed the outfit away on the wagon seat. I barely got my arms out of the coat sleeves when he charged, his hamlike fist catching me on the side of my head. I saw pinwheels of fire, and fell heavily.

Before I could get back to my feet, his boot thudded into my ribs, and excruciating pain lanced through my whole body. In desperation, I grabbed the foot and twisted over onto my back, drawing up my legs. Lashing out with both of my feet, I caught him full in the chest, and sent him crashing to the ground with a strangled squawk.

I managed to get up on one knee before he charged again. Every breath was like a knife in my side, so I knew at least one rib was broken. As he came lumbering in, I rose up suddenly, butting him in the throat with my head, then wrapping both arms around his waist as we fell together.

He thrashed around, catching me in the face with an edge of his hand. I felt the skin split, and the blood poured across my face. Half blinded, I reached out, groping, and hooked a thumb in the corner of his mouth, tearing his cheek. With a shriek, he scrabbled in the dirt, trying to get away from me.

Gasping, I got to my feet and pawed at the blood with my sleeve. Sim was standing, feeling in wonderment at his torn cheek. Then, mouthing curses, he charged at me again, fists flailing, a look of insane fury on his face.

I stood my ground, feinting with a right and dropping my left shoulder. Then, as he struck at me, I hit him with the left, hard as I could, full in the face. I felt teeth give and he was driven to the ground.

As he managed to get up on one knee, I grabbed a handhold in his greasy hair, and brought one up from the ground, hitting him square on the point of his chin. He shuddered and collapsed in the dirt. My eyes seeing red, I grabbed at his shirtfront and smashed my fist into his face, while he lolled helplessly, his mouth slack. Then I let him drop to the ground, and stood up, swaying. Weariness swept over me, and I almost fell.

A voice spoke, almost in my ear, and an arm went about my shoulders. It was Bob Wright.

"It's all over now, Frank. He's had all he can take. We better get inside, and take a look at your face. You're all bloody. I'll send somebody for Doc McCarty."

I retrieved my gun belt, and buckled it around my waist. A number of bystanders were gawking at us from the street, and several shouted that I'd done a good job. I took my neckerchief from around my neck and wiped some of the blood away, then carefully fitted my new hat on my head, and reached out for my coat. Wright took it out of my hand and started for the storefront.

Blackbeard was on his feet, looking around dazedly, leaning on the tailboard of the wagon. Sim was stirring, and he rolled over on his belly trying to get his hands under him. His face was a mask of blood; and as we watched, he coughed, and spat tooth fragments out of his torn mouth.

"What time's it getting to be?" I asked Wright. "I gotta help Tilghman with the race."

He fished his watch out of his pocket, and consulted it a moment. "Twenty minutes before two," he answered. "You got time enough. First off, we have to get you cleaned up. The Marshal won't appreciate seeing you like this. He's a great one for neatness." He laughed....

CHAPTER
FOURTEEN

MCARTY CAME, ALL right, but he grumbled at being summoned from the race just as it was ready to begin. When he found out I was the patient and heard what I'd done to his enemy, old Blackbeard, he calmed down.

"Good for you, young man," he told me. "Too bad you have scruples about shooting unarmed scoundrels, like those two."

He had me in a chair, Wright's clerk standing by, a basin of warm water in his hands. After he'd gotten the blood off my face, he peered at the gash in my cheek.

"Hmmm. Might be a good idea to take a stitch or two, and close that up tightly. Otherwise you're going to have a bad scar there, Mr. Specter." He turned to Bob Wright.

"Don't you have whiskey in this store, Mr. Wright? A man can't take stitches without a drop of spirits. Come! Come! Let's not take all day! Must see that race. My money is on the black man, and I want to see that he gets a fair shake."

Wright went hurrying off, and returned a short

time later with a straw-wrapped bottle which he handed to McCarty.

Tearing off the wrappings, McCarty gasped and held it up for all of us to see. "I asked for whiskey," he said. "And he brings me liquid gold! Look! Dant's Pendennis Club! We are rubbing elbows with a wealthy man, my friends.... Where," he asked, "where did you come by such a treasure?"

Wright looked at him, puzzled by his reaction. "Why, the last bull train that come through here, before the railroad, that is. Feller on the train traded me four cases for a new Marlin rifle. I threw in two boxes of cartridges, because I figured I'd got the best of the deal."

"Well, I should say you did! Before I leave here, I want to make a purchase. At least a case, or more if you care to part with it."

"Now, let's get this man fixed up, so we can get back and watch the race." He offered me the bottle, after prying out the cork, and I took a generous swallow. It was smooth, far different from the whiskeys sold over most bars.

Doc took two stitches in my cheek, with helpings from the bottle before, after, and during the operation. A strip of court plaster was used to cover the wound, and I was as good as new! I paid him the dollar he said was normal for house calls, and he left after negotiating with Bob Wright.

I bought a new shirt and neckerchief, and changed clothes in the stock room. Glancing in a mirror, I decided I didn't look too bad to appear in public. The court plaster was not exactly a match for my sun-browned face, but it gave no hint of the nasty gash underneath.

Bob, the clerk, and I left together. I thanked them both for the kindness they'd shown me. Wright waved it off with a gesture, and the clerk said it was all part of his job. I promised myself I'd do something for them, if I had an opportunity. We strolled on down to the depot platform, where my friends Bill and Bat were holding forth.

When we arrived, the two contestants were just on the way to the starting point, three hundred yards downtrack. Hogan was barefoot, wearing a thin pair of trousers and an undershirt, while Sawyer boasted a pair of thin-soled shoes, with red flannel underwear covering his frame. An attempt at modesty had been achieved with a pair of cut-off pants over his shanks.

Ford County Sheriff Pat Sughrue was to act as the starter, and he was hollering for the contestants to take their place on the starting line. The crowd added their encouragements, some of them profane, and both men were trotting now.

Tilghman glanced at my face and asked what'd kept me. I told him I'd tell him all about it when the race was over.

"Where do you want me to stand?" I asked him. "What's my job here?"

"When those two finish the race," he told me, "I want to be sure the crowd doesn't swarm all over 'em. The ones that lose on the race are liable to murder the winner. Just you station yourself on the other side of the tracks, and hustle them both over here to the platform."

There were some tools laying on a baggage cart, and among them a pick. I knocked out the handle and took it with me, to the other side of the tracks....

A moment later, a six-gun roared, and the race began. I had to force the bystanders back, as they swarmed out on the track directly in the path of the runners.

"C'mon folks," I urged. "Give those boys some room. The race can't be finished if you're blocking the track."

There was some grumbling, but they did move. Far away in the distance, I could see two tiny figures moving toward us, growing bigger by the second. The crowds were following on the tracks behind them, some almost keeping up the pace. My arms were outstretched, with the pick handle menacing a press of bystanders crowded against me.

Now they were much closer, and it seemed they were almost neck and neck. A hundred yards to go, and they were straining! I could see cords standing out on both their necks, as each made a convulsive effort to outdistance the other. The black man ran loose-jointedly, his arms akimbo, while Sawyer pumped away, arms and legs in rhythmical precision, his head held high, and his mouth wide open!

Now they were only thirty yards from the finish line, and Hogan had taken a slight lead! His neck outstretched and a grim smile on his tightly closed mouth, he was steadily drawing away from the gasping Sawyer....

The crowd was screaming in my ear as they swept down the track, Hogan ahead by at least three feet! Then they flashed by, and the race was over. Hogan was the winner!

Quickly, I ran toward the two, whose pace had slowed now to a loose-jointed stagger. Grabbing them by the upper arms, I rushed them across the tracks and up onto the platform.

Tilghman and Masterson were right there, six-guns in hand, and both fired in the air. The thunderous roar brought that bunch to a halt, right away, and the crowd started to mill in circles, keeping far back from the depot platform.

Tilghman clapped Hogan on the back. "Good job,

Bill." He turned to me. "And you too, Frank. Looked like that herd was out for blood."

"Well! What do you think of our winner, here? Never did see anything like that in my life! Walked right away, without so much as an aye, yes, or kiss my rear! Yessir Bill, I gotta hand it to you. You ran a fine race.... And you, too," he told Sawyer. "You're both good boys. We gotta do this again, some day. Maybe in some other town..."

Masterson looked up, a smile on his face. "How about you and me coming up with some sort of consolation prize for our Mr. Sawyer? He ran a good race, like you said, and we won a nice piece of change for ourselves. Say, about two hundred. That's just a hundred apiece. We can afford that, and it'll make Mr. Sawyer a lot happier."

Tilghman agreed, and they each gave him a sheaf of bills. A few moments later, Sheriff Sughrue came up, and we went to the Long Branch, where Hogan was presented with the winner's prize. One thousand dollars in cash.

"What're you gonna do with all that money?" Bat asked him. "You got enough there to get yourself set up in some sort of business. Or mebbe buy yourself a small farm. What're your plans, Bill?"

Hogan grinned. "Well, right now I'm gonna git myself a bath. Then I'm gonna go down to Mr. Wright's store and buy me the purtiest dress he's got in that place. A brand new dress for my lady fr'en. Somethin' with lots of bright red, and greens, and purples! Like no dress she's done ever seen before! Then, I'm gonna take her that dress, and I'm gittin' down on my knees, and pro-posin' a question to that lady...."

He grinned, and rolled his eyes. "I'm gonna marry up with that lady, and then...we'll look for that farm!"

We all had a good laugh, including Bill Hogan. With that thousand dollars tucked away, he thanked everyone and shook hands all around. A mighty cheer went up as he pranced out the door, waving his arms and still laughing.

It had been quite a day for me, and I was really tired. A good night's sleep would help a lot, I thought to myself. I was also obliged to make some plans for the future. Judah's kindness was appreciated, but I couldn't go on cowboying for the rest of my life. I was remembering more and more of the past, and part of that was tied up with Pinkerton's Agency.

Bill Pinkerton had told me that the trip to Santa Fe need not be taken. The man they had sent me to see was dead. A horse had rolled on him, and he'd actually been killed, even before I'd left Chicago to see him. Well, they'd find another job for me, I was certain of that....

Tilghman nudged me.... I realized he'd been talking to me all along, and I hadn't heard.

"What was that, Bill?" I asked.

"I said you looked like you were miles away. Thinking about your future, ain't you? Well, I wouldn't worry. You're welcome to the deputy's job, if you want it."

"Thanks, Bill. I appreciate that. But I reckon I'll be moving on again, soon. Lots of places I've never been. You know, I'm going to miss this part of the country. Even with getting knocked in the head and not knowing who I was, it's been a happy time for me."

"We'll all miss you too, Frank. Judah most of all. That feller thinks a whole lot of you, whether you know it or not. Then there's the roundup, this fall. He'll be short-handed, with Sim not working there any more. Judah said you were as good as any man with that cuttin' horse, Amigo."

"Oh! Well, that is a fine horse. Most any man'd look as if he knew what he was doing with a fine horse like that under him. I worked with cows, when I was younger. Reckon it stays with a man. Right now, I believe I'll head for home."

I shoved back my chair and stood up. Then, remembering, I unpinned the badge and handed it to Tilghman.

"Any time you're needful of an extra deputy, you know how to find me, Bill. See you boys later."

When I was almost to the door, a voice stopped me in my tracks. The voice spoke again, the words somewhat garbled, like the owner had a sore mouth....

"I said I'm gonna kill you, Specter!"

Slowly, I turned around, my hands held wide from my body. Sim stood against the bar, his hand poised, clawlike, over a holstered Colt. His head was hunched forward, his neck muscles corded with strain.

"Can't you hear good, mister? I said I'm gonna blow yore guts out. Now draw! Damn yuh, draw!"

My hands still well clear of my body, I faced him, silently. He was wound up like a clock. Probably took him hours just to work his courage up to this point.

"Sim," I said quietly. "I got no more quarrel with you. We settled our differences this afternoon. Now back off; we have nothing here that's worth killing a man over."

He sneered. "So! The big, bad gunfighter's gonna crawfish, is he? I figgered you was mostly show. But you got another think comin', you have. You better draw, 'cause I'll kill you like a dog, with or without a gun in yore hand!"

Carefully, I moved my hands to the center of my belt. It came unbuckled in my hand. Silently, I handed my rig to the bartender, who had been serving a table nearby.

"I'll be back for that, tomorrow," I told him.

Ignoring Simpkins, I reached up and pushed at the doors, swinging them wide open. Someone yelled; it could have been Tilghman. A six-gun boomed, and a white-hot pain streaked across the top of my left shoulder. Sim was cursing, and his gun boomed again, this time missing me completely.

Whirling around, my hands reached out, and the derringers blazed away. Sim's hand went to his throat, where a gout of blood had suddenly appeared. He was choking.... His gun had slipped from nerveless fingers, and he was sinking, his hand clutching his throat, and blood gushing between his fingers.

Tilghman was at my side in a bound, Masterson right there also. Bat had his Colt out, and motioned everyone to remain right where they were.

Blood was welling out of a tear in the coat, and my shoulder was a little stiff. I turned the barrels on the Wessons, and put them back into their compartments. Reaching over, I took my rig away from the bartender, and strapped it on.

"You're hit," said Tilghman. "Is it bad?"

"Just a scratch," I told him. "Nothing a little soap and water won't cure. How about this, Bill? Will I be charged? I gave him every chance to back out. I didn't want to shoot the poor devil!"

"Not a chance," he replied. "Self-defense, in front of a couple dozen witnesses. Why'd you do it, Frank? Givin' him an edge, like you did? Turning around like that, and givin' up your belt gun. Why? You're luckier than a six-toed cat! If that skunk had been a better shot, you'd be deader'n hell right now!"

"Bill," I looked him square in the eye. "My reputation's not an easy thing to live with, believe me. Every time this happens, that reputation grows, and grows, and like the fish stories you hear, it gains a lot in the telling. Some folks claim I've killed forty or fifty men, and I haven't, but you can't stop folks from telling these stories. You surely got your own records inflated, haven't you? And you, Bat. When was the last time you had some stranger look at you, fear in his eyes, because of your reputation? No! It's not an easy thing to live with, but the world needs men like us. Men to police this world of ours, and kill the few who try to ruin it for the many. 'Nuff said. I'm going home!"

Outside the door waited the surprise of my life! It was Nancy, sitting up on the seat of that wagon we'd bought from Bob Wright. On the seat beside her was a fellow wearing a big white hat, blue jeans, and a brushjacket. It was White Wolf! Behind him was Sun Bird, dressed in gingham, with an unusually wide bonnet framing her pretty face. Judah was on the ground next to the wagon, a big grin wreathing his face.

"Howdy do, Mr. Specter," said Nancy. "May I present some friends of mine? This is Tom Wolfe, and his wife, Birdie."

"Well I never..." What could I say? I reached out, awkwardly, and shook hands, unsure whether to laugh or make some remark or what. Like I'd said before, living with Nancy would be one surprise situation after another....

"Well," said Nancy. "Are you gonna just stand there? We got better things to do than to hang around Dodge City! It may just interest you to know that we're headed for Wyoming Territory. Take a look at the wagon cover!"

I did, and in addition to HEADED HOME, it had other words inked in below. Specifically, TO WYOMING.

"My horse," I said, finally. "I got to get my horse. It won't take but a minute. He's tied up on the other side..."

"He's tied on behind, along with my mare. Now c'mon! We ain't got all day! I'll climb in the back with Birdie. You can ride up here on the seat with Tom."

"But, your dad! How...We gotta...married..."

"My dad knows all about everything. He helped me get the two of them away from the cave. Dad found the cave, after I had given up, and even cut Tom's hair. So, you see, he's on our side, and he agrees we should leave Dodge, and now!"

"As for us getting married, you'd better believe we'll do that! There's a preacher in Julesburg, and since we're following the western cattle trail, we'll be passing through. I know there's a preacher here in Dodge, but this town's not a healthy place for folks like Tom and Birdie. So, c'mon! We got miles to cover yet today!"

I looked up at her, then over to Judah. He shrugged, but with a smile on his face....We shook hands....

"Aw hell, Tom," I said. "Move on over...."

News item:

Dodge City *Globe*, June 24, 1884,
Dodge City, Kansas.

A three-hundred-yard foot race for a purse of $1000, between a white man named Sawyer and a colored man named Hogan, of this city, took place last Saturday afternoon [June 21] on the railroad track below the depot. Hogan won the race, by about three feet, and deceived a great many, who had their money up on the white man. Over three hundred people turned out to witness the race, among whom were quite a fair sprinkling of the fair Demimonde. "Bat" and "Til" [William M. Tilghman] were the judges; therefore, everything was on the square, and no grumbling was heard by the losers.

AUTHOR'S NOTE

THE PRINCIPAL CHARACTER in this novel, Frank Specter, AKA Joe Warner, is based on a little-known but highly proficient gunfighter, Mr. Frank Canton. Born Joe Horner in 1849, this man killed a Negro trooper of the Sixth U.S. Cavalry, wounding his companion and fleeing Jacksboro, Texas, in 1874. Though born Joe Horner, he changed his name to Frank Canton sometime between 1874 and 1877, and remained Canton to the end.

Frank Canton went on to become a sheriff several times; he was involved in the Johnson County War in Wyoming; he served as a deputy sheriff more than once; was a deputy U.S. marshal in the Alaskan Gold Rush; again a deputy U.S. marshal in Oklahoma during the U.S. Marshal E.D. Nix administration.

Was appointed adjutant-general of the Oklahoma National Guard in 1907, where he served with distinction for ten years with the rank of major general. He passed away in 1927, aged seventy-eight.

Incidents portrayed in this novel are entirely fictitious and were never experienced by Mr. Canton.

ROBERT VAUGHN BELL
Creek Park Ranch
February 4, 1982

About the Author

Born in Omaha, Nebraska, in 1924, Robert Bell's earliest ambition was to become a rodeo clown. Since then, he has experienced a multifaceted career—as a parachutist during World War II, a telephone lineman, gunsmith, salvage diver, deputy sheriff, seaman, and most recently, a cattle rancher. In addition, Bell has written numerous magazine articles and considers himself an historian.

Bell resides on his ranch with his wife in Garden Valley, California.

Ride into the world of adventure with Ballantine's western novels!

Available at your bookstore or use this coupon.

____ APACHE WELLS by Robert Steelman   29067   1.75
They carved a home out of the desert—with blood.

____ DAKOTA TERRITORY by Robert Steelman   28852   1.75
He left his fancy learning back East, and got a new education out West.

____ FOLLOW THE FREE WIND, Leigh Brackett   29008   1.75
A mountain man more legend than fact, more truth than myth.

____ HOMBRE, Elmore Leonard   28850   1.75
"One of the Twenty-five best westerns of all time!" Western Writers of America.

____ DEATHWIND by James Powell   28648   1.75
They sentenced him unjustly to jail. When he came out, he sentenced them to death.

BALLANTINE MAIL SALES
Dept. AL, 201 E. 50th St., New York, N.Y. 10022

Please send me the BALLANTINE or DEL REY BOOKS I have checked above. I am enclosing $ _____ (add 50¢ per copy to cover postage and handling). Send check or money order — no cash or C.O.D.'s please. Prices and numbers are subject to change without notice.

Name_____

Address_____

City_____ State_____ Zip Code_____

07   Allow at least 4 weeks for delivery.   AL-22